WONDER WOMAN

Wonder Woman: The Official Movie Novelization
Print edition ISBN: 9781785653780
E-book edition ISBN: 9781785653797

Published by Titan Books
A division of Titan Publishing Group Ltd
144 Southwark Street, London SE1 0UP

First edition: June 2017
10 9 8 7 6 5 4 3 2 1

This book is a work of fiction. Any references to historical events, real people, or real places are used fictitiously. Other names, characters, places, and events are products of the author's imagination, and any resemblance to actual events or places or persons, living or dead, is entirely coincidental. The publisher does not have any control over and does not assume any responsibility for author or third-party websites or their content.

A CIP catalogue record for this title is available from the British Library.

Printed and bound in the USA.

WONDER WOMAN

Directed by **PATTY JENKINS**
Story by **ZACK SNYDER & ALLAN HEINBERG** AND **JASON FUCHS**
Screenplay by **ALLAN HEINBERG**
Based on the character created by
WILLIAM MOULTON MARSTON
Novelization by **NANCY HOLDER**

TITAN BOOKS

A shimmering blue planet hangs in space.
On it lives a true hero of the people.
She is a legend, feared by some, beloved by others.
It is her sacred duty to defend the world.

*"The bravest are surely those who have the
clearest vision of what is before them, glory
and danger alike, and yet notwithstanding,
go out to meet it."*
—Thucydides (460 BC–395 BC)

"*I used to want to save the world. This beautiful place. But I knew so little then. It is a land of beauty and wonder, worth cherishing in every way. But the closer you get, the more you see the great darkness simmering within. And mankind?*
Mankind is another story altogether.

What one does when faced with the truth is more difficult than you think.

I learned this the hard way a long, long time ago. And now, I will never be the same."

—Diana, Princess of
Themyscira

BOOK I

AMAZON

"If you want peace, prepare for war."
—Publius Flavis Vegetius Renatus
(4th century)

1

Paris, France
The Present

It was a crisp Paris morning, a breeze off the Seine river offering freshly baked croissants and coffee, the thrumming buzz and blare of traffic promising a busy day. Draped in a red coat straight out of *Paris Vogue*, her dark hair wrapped in a sleek chignon, Diana Prince turned briskly down Paris's Cour Napoléon, her high heels clicking on the ribbed pavement. To her left was the elegant Café Marly, to the right the I.M. Pei glass and metal pyramid that adorned the entry courtyard of the famous Louvre Museum, home of, among other treasures, the Mona Lisa. In black berets, bullet-proof vests, and camouflage fatigues, armed soldiers patrolled. Their FAMAS assault rifles seemed jarringly out of place against the backdrop of an icon of modern art and the ornate sixteenth-century palace.

The presence of military security to thwart terrorist threats was a recent development, but it was not the first time armed soldiers had patrolled the square. During World War II, the City of Light had fallen under the boots of Nazi invaders, and the irreplaceable treasures of one of the world's greatest museums had been looted and shipped back to Germany.

The world still had much to learn about what was truly valuable. Nothing was more precious than life. But that simple concept seemed difficult to grasp.

Out of Diana's range of vision, an armored delivery truck marked Wayne Enterprises pulled up to the museum entrance. Uniformed officers carefully unloaded a small black security case, also stamped with the logo of the Gotham-based international conglomerate owned by a man who, like Diana, led a double life.

After showing her ID badge to the guard at the main entrance, she put her purse and briefcase on the conveyor belt to be scanned. There was no line at the checkpoint. The museum would not open to the public for another two hours. As he did every day, the guard tried to flirt with her as he handed her back her belongings. She knew he thought she was a native Parisienne, which was probably the greatest compliment he as a Parisian could offer. He would be astonished if he knew how many languages she spoke fluently. As always, she smiled, politely nodded her thanks, and quickly moved on.

The cleaning staff had done their work the night before: the museum was spotless and all but deserted. Diana walked a familiar path over gleaming marble floors, through the sequence of empty adjoining salons. The scale of the rooms—particularly the ceiling height— was most impressive, as had been intended. Renaissance palaces such as this were designed to instill awe and to reflect the might of the occupants. With the monarchs long gone, the great Musée now reflected the power and sensibilities of the French people.

To reach her office she had to pass through the Richelieu Wing and the Department of Near Eastern Antiquities. On either side of the aisle, glass-cased, spotlighted Assyrian bas-reliefs revealed fragments of the history of a three-thousand-year-old civilization: its great cultural accomplishments, but also the pitched battles it had won, the taking of prisoners, mass deportations of conquered peoples, and the fall of competing empires.

The frosted glass of her office door was emblazoned in gold letters: DIANA PRINCE, CURATOR, DEPARTMENT OF ANTIQUITIES. The interior space on the other side was filled by a desk and display cases of the early Greek artifacts she was in the process of cataloguing. Ancient weapons of war lined the shelves: axes, bows and arrows, and several versions of the short sword called *xiphos*—customarily only drawn after a warrior's spear broke. There were daggers, slings for stones and lead pellets, body armor, leather-covered wooden shields, and metal helmets of both the Chalcidian—foot soldier—and Boeotian—cavalry—varieties. As it happened, every ancient piece in the collection was similar to something she had either wielded herself, or had seen in the armory on Themyscira. Gifts from the Gods, as her mother had called them.

She had no more than set her purse down beside the desk when a soft knock sounded on the doorjamb. A uniformed deliveryman held out a valise. When she saw the logo on the side it gave her pause; the case was not from another museum or gallery, but Wayne Enterprises. Bruce Wayne. They had crossed paths recently, to put it mildly. In fact, together with a third friend of justice, they had put an end to Doomsday. Literally.

She signed for the delivery, then waited until she was alone before opening the lid of the case.

And there it was. Nestled in protective packing was a sepia-toned daguerreotype photograph of a handful of five people posed on a pile of broken bricks at the edge of a muddy village square. In that moment, she stood once again amid the rubble left by a German artillery barrage, shield and sword in hand, wreathed in the caustic perfume of wet, charred wood and burned cordite. A moment of triumph frozen in time, shared by the four unsmiling, heavily armed men who bracketed her. Though the monochrome photo couldn't show it, the eyes of the man standing to her right had been intensely blue, as blue as the sea that surrounded Themyscira, the island of her birth. Feelings of tenderness and pride and loss suddenly welled up, hitting her hard. The five of them had had to stand very still for the photographer's camera—hence their unsmiling faces. But they had been so happy then, in that moment of victory and celebration in the midst of chaos. That sweet, lost moment; those dear, lost warriors.

Though she had made peace with mortality: Steve Trevor, dearest of all.

She picked up the enclosed note. It was unsigned, but she recognized the handwriting. Bruce Wayne's.

"I found the original. Maybe one day you'll tell me your story."

Surrounded by history, once more Diana took in the smudged faces of heroes long dead, and her own face, unchanged despite the passing of so many years. A century. The image captured more than just an instant in time. It held an elemental kernel of truth: how Wonder Woman came to be.

2

The Island of Themyscira
In the Gods' Own Time

"Diana!" Mnemosyne cried, her head popping up from the bushes like a dormouse. "Come back here!"

Busted! Diana, tiny Princess of Themyscira, poured on more speed as she dashed away from the scene of the crime. Surely Mnemosyne *had* to know that there were other things to do on a day like this than sit in a room and learn about the Peloponnesian War. Who needed to learn about human beings? She had never even met one in her entire life—eight years, by mortal count—and doubted she ever would.

In a dress of the palest gold and a tan leather decorative harness in the Amazonian style, with her silver and gold arm guards, Diana beat her retreat. As she capered along a path of white stone, the sea sparkled, begging to be swum in. The breeze demanded a kite. The tower spires of swirling rock looped with hanging vines, the terraces of grapes and olives, and sturdy, slender footbridges crossing waterfalls and canyons insisted that she saddle her pony and explore the vast paradise that was her home.

She burst into the busy square where Amazons were buying and selling a cornucopia of goods: fragrant cheese, olive oil, delicious bread; dried fish and game; bracelets, pottery, and weapons. Amazons loved their weapons. Banners flapped; chickens clucked. Everyone was happy to see her, calling out "Good morning, Diana!" "Hello, Princess!"

She chugged along merrily, aware that her escape attempt was really just a game. For Diana to win, Mnemosyne had to decide it was just too much trouble to catch her rebellious student and that she'd try again tomorrow. After all, that had worked before.

Mnemosyne was not Diana's first tutor.

The marketplace left in the dust, she trotted along a ledge and to her delight, realized she'd reached the Amazon training ground. The natural amphitheater—a grassy field bordered on three sides by exposed boulders and shelves of gray rock, and on the fourth by a cliff opening onto the wide blue sea—was filled with clashing bodies, lithe and powerful. In the center, overseeing the organized chaos, strode the Amazons' great general, Antiope—Diana's aunt. Antiope wore her tiara and armor with regal bearing and with her long blond hair, now braided, she looked like Diana's mother the Queen, except that Diana had never seen her mother in battle.

A dozen different struggles played out simultaneously, some one on one, others more lopsided—two, three, five on one. The weapons were ancient, powered by muscle, sinew, and bone. Thrilled, Diana shadowed their movements as swords clanged and *bō* staves thwacked. Hair flying, two figures on horseback charged each other across the rock-strewn meadow, wielding spears and shields. They wore metal breastplates, leather shoulder guards, and the short ornamental leather fringe at their waists that the Greeks called *pteruges*. They flung themselves into the air, twirling and spiraling twenty, thirty, a hundred feet, arching and contorting as they fell fearlessly back to earth. Leaping off their horses, flinging themselves from the pommel, they grabbed up swords off the ground, javelins; an amphora met its end with the fierce toss of spear and discharged its load of dirt.

Mighty Artemis stood on a revolving wooden platform, taking on all comers. The dark-skinned Amazon rippled with muscles as she parried and thrusted with her sword. Oh, to be like Artemis!

All the combatants on the field were female and in the bursting prime of their lives. They hacked and slashed, putting their mighty force into their moves, but there was no spilled blood or bodies sprawled on the grass. These Amazons had sparred against each other for so long that they could go all out without injuring each other—at least, not permanently. They were relentless and unyielding. Proud, noble, and strong.

Now *this* was something worth learning. To fight among them as a sister in arms. To stand unopposed on the field of combat. Once she could fight she would be all grown up, a woman and a true Amazon, done with sitting still in classrooms. The Spartans defeated the Greeks in the Peloponnesian War. Boom. Done.

Look out! she silently called to an Amazon, as her attacker leaped from her horse with her sword held high. But the great warrior easily deflected the overhead swing of her assailant's blade. Her foe executed a forward roll to put distance between herself and her quarry, moving with the grace of a cheetah.

Diana shadowed each movement, punching, kicking, blowing air from her rosy cheeks, still chubby with the last traces of baby fat. Oh, how she wanted to be swept up in the middle of the whirlwind, to spin and grunt and shout and be a champion.

On the far side of the meadow, a pair of riders towed a target on wheels down a narrow track. One hundred yards away, a line of archers let arrows fly, one by one. The dark arrows disappeared into the clear sky and reappeared as they fell in a perfect arc to strike the rapidly moving straw target. The flight of arrows was followed by a rain of javelins as the moving target reversed direction. They were much easier to follow with the naked eye and when they slammed into and through the target, they rocked it on its wheels and sent up a puff of dust.

Then Diana turned her attention to the armored warriors exercising their close-combat fighting skills. Now her Aunt Antiope keenly observed the fiery warrior Menalippe as she demolished her challenger's strategic attack. The general's muscles were like steel, her arms wrapped in leather, and boots up to her thighs. Her distinctive tiara, an inverted triangle decorated with a sunburst banded in different kinds of metals, caught the light.

Not twenty feet away, Artemis, one of the most skilled of all the Amazon warriors, was locked in combat with Eliana. Their swords clashed, ringing through the air. Sparks flew. Their boots kicked up divots of grass. As the fighters circled, each was looking for a weakness, a point of attack. When Artemis found it, things happened very quickly. And decisively. If Diana had blinked, she would have missed it. First a feint that drew her opponent forward, then a backspin that put her behind Eliana's hip and shield hand.

Frozen for a split-second, Eliana couldn't bring sword or shield across her body to defend. She had to pivot to do that. As Eliana's right foot left the ground, Artemis was already rearing back, drawing her knee to her chest, and with the sole of her foot kicked her square in the behind. Because Eliana was off balance it wouldn't have taken much of a kick to send her to the ground, but Artemis didn't hold back an ounce of her power, and the impact sent the other woman flying through the air, landing and skidding on her face and hands over the grass. In the process, she lost her sword and some of her dignity.

Antiope ticked her gaze over to Diana. Maybe she *tried* to narrow her eyes in disapproval, but Diana saw the smile behind her *why aren't you with Mnemosyne* look. She shot the general an answering look that said, *Because I'm ready to fight. Let me try!*

"Diana! I see you!" her tutor shouted at her back.

Uh-oh. Diana tamped down a giggle and took off again. Though the tutor was catching up, this was a legendary foot race indeed. Reveling in the thrill of the chase, she ran on, charging up a hill, happy as a baboon. Wily Mnemosyne caught sight of her and Diana coursed down another walkway, maybe a little too fast, and then she launched herself toward another path below. She imagined herself soaring through the air just like the warriors—except that the pathway was *just* a little bit farther down than she'd assumed—

My worst idea. Maybe my last!

Then something caught her by the arm and with a gentle upward jerk, stopped her fall.

21

She hung suspended by her mother's hand, caught and held as if she weighed nothing. Those strong fingers had plaited her hair only this morning. A gleaming gauntlet, symbol of the wearer's power. Diana gazed up at her mother, who sat on horseback, magnificent and queenly. Hippolyta's long unbound sun-streaked hair was held in place by her tiara, and her muscular arms were wrapped in leather. She was every inch a warrior. And at the moment, a mother who had caught her daughter playing hooky.

As innocently as she could, Diana smiled up at her sweetly and said, "Hello, Mother. How are you today?"

Queen Hippolyta nodded, unable to completely hide a smile. "Let's get you back to school before another tutor quits."

She's not mad, Diana thought. *I think she's actually pretty impressed.* She decided to push a little bit. "But, Mother… don't you think it's time to start my training?"

Her mother pulled her up, sat her on the front of the saddle, and embraced her. Diana was certain that her mother was going to agree. *Finally.*

Just then Antiope came riding up to meet them with Artemis at her side. Diana figured that Antiope would stick up for her. After all, her aunt had seen her mimicking her battle moves perfectly.

Well, almost perfectly.

When she caught the general's eye, she brightened and blurted out, "*Antiope* thinks I'm ready."

"Does she?" Hippolyta said, turning a measured gaze onto the island's military leader.

Antiope approached the queen's steed, head lowered out of deference. Raising her gaze to meet Hippolyta's, she said, "I could begin showing her some things…"

Yes! Diana exulted. *Yes, yes, yes!*

The queen's silence in response to the offer was deafening. Her horse shied a bit, sidestepping, and she reined it in. Still, silence was not a "no." Maybe she was thinking it over.

"She should at least be able to defend herself," Antiope persisted. That was right, absolutely right.

"From whom?"

Monkeys in the forest, Diana thought of replying, although she had never actually seen a monkey in the forest. Or anywhere, for that matter. *Peacocks, then. Evil peacocks. We have a lot of peacocks.*

"In the event of an invasion," Antiope said with conviction.

Spartans!

"Isn't that why I have the greatest warrior in our history leading an entire army, General?" the queen asked with the same tone of voice she used while pointing out to Diana that muddy arms and legs did not belong in the bed of a princess when the bathing pool was nearby. Or that surely vegetables were just as important to a growing body as honey cakes.

Antiope said, "I pray a day will never come where she has to fight, but you know that a scorpion must sting, a wolf must hunt…"

"She's a child. The only child on the island. Please, let her be so." The queen's words were gentle but firm. Diana wanted to groan with frustration. Still, like any good Amazon, she wasn't about to give up without a fight.

"But, Mother," she protested.

"There will be no training," Hippolyta declared, closing

the discussion. Then the queen effortlessly swung Diana around behind her on the saddle and told her horse to go. As the mount obeyed—because who didn't obey Hippolyta, Queen of the Amazons?—Diana turned and looked back at Antiope. The general's quick, confident nod seemed not just a goodbye, but a covert reassurance. Diana raised her brows. Did it mean she *would* help her train?

Then mother and daughter headed to the prison of very old wars and lists of dates that had nothing to do with *now*. But perhaps there was hope after all?

Night. The gentle crashing of the waves; fireflies and wishing stars; the hoot of an owl.

The night watch was set, the moon was out, and Diana couldn't help but fidget as her mother brushed her hair. She kept thinking about Antiope's quick nod. Training, battling, victory! Being a real Amazon and not everybody's favorite (and only) baby. Antiope was going to make it happen, and soon.

She fidgeted some more, barely able to keep still. There was absolutely no way she would be able to sleep tonight. She would toss and turn as if she were on a boat. Her bed in the palace was set into the wall, in a carved alcove that had always reminded her of a cross between a shield and a seashell. The polished stone of the floor gleamed, reflecting candlelight and fires in braziers in niches. Most nights she loved this ritual, sitting in her lovely bed while her mother tended her, then snuggling up to dream of forthcoming battles and adventures. But tonight was another matter.

"What if I promised to be careful?" Diana pleaded.

The queen smoothed Diana's hair, fingers lingering among the strands. "It's time to sleep," she said tenderly.

There had to be *some* way Diana could convince her. "What if I didn't use a sword?"

"Fighting doesn't make you a hero."

Her mother was missing the point entirely. Or maybe not quite entirely. It would be lovely to be a hero. But it would be even lovelier to go into close combat with Artemis.

"Just a shield then. No sharp edges."

Hippolyta gazed at Diana with a gentle but earnest expression as Diana lay back on her pillow. "Diana," she said, "you are the most precious thing in this world to me. I wished for you so much, so I sculpted you from clay myself and begged Zeus to give you life."

Diana huffed and pulled the covers up to her chin. "You've *told* me that story." Still, it was a very nice story.

"Then I will tell you a new one. One of our people, and my days of battle," Hippolyta said.

Diana's face lit up. Her mother's prowess in battle was legendary. She was the fiercest Amazon on the entire island—even fiercer than Antiope.

She sat up as her mother crossed to a table, picking up what appeared to be a large leather folder embossed with metal that had been lying beside a candle. Hippolyta came back to the bed. The folder was exquisitely decorated with an intricate design that reminded Diana of Antiope's tiara. She watched carefully as her mother prepared to open it.

For her part, Hippolyta, Queen of the Amazons, mother of the only child on Themyscira, wondered—as she had so often before—if she was doing the right thing. To successfully guide and guard her people, a Queen must appear sure of herself. The mantle of authority, no matter how heavy, hung on her shoulders alone. She had led her people out of bondage so very long ago, and they still looked to her for leadership and guidance. Zeus had willed it so. But she and Zeus had also willed other things…

She frowned at Diana's show of misplaced interest—dreaming of glory as any young warrior would, unaware of the terrible toll that true war took on life and spirit. Time to make her aware, then. "So you will finally understand… why *war* is nothing to hope for."

Then the Queen opened the cover, revealing a stylized triptych of images against shimmering backdrops. At the top of one panel the magnificent Gods and Goddesses looked down from the lofty heavens of Mt. Olympus, their mysterious domain swaddled in clouds and mist. All praise to the Gods, givers of music, art, harmony, and love.

"Long ago," Hippolyta said, "when time was new, and all of history was still a dream, the Gods ruled the Earth, Zeus king among them." He reigned supreme, the giver of life. The father of all.

Diana waited for the good part.

"Zeus created beings over which the Gods would rule," the queen told her. "Beings born in his image—fair and good, strong and passionate. He called his creation 'man.'"

Against a lush landscape of forest, field, and pasture, men, women, and children took form. They carried baskets of food and smiled at one another. Some lounged together on the earth, savoring the gifts of the Gods.

"And mankind was good," Hippolyta continued.

Diana was enchanted. The women looked like

Amazons. The men resembled women somewhat, but there were marked differences. She would like to meet a man one day. But there were none on their island—and no other children, either. Just her. But like the Amazons, these people appeared to be very happy, strong, and confident.

"But one of the Gods grew envious of Zeus's love for mankind," Hippolyta continued, "and sought to corrupt his creation."

Above, on Olympus, a shadowy figure in a horned helmet loomed from dark gray clouds, menacingly surveying the humans below. "This was Ares, the God of War. Ares poisoned men's hearts with suspicion, vengeance, and rage. He turned them against one another," Hippolyta continued.

Diana's eyes widened as she watched groups of people clump together, turning into armies. Then the armies turned on each other, until all the little Amazon could see was an enormous battlefield littered with the dying and the dead. It would be a shocking thing to show any child, but this was *her* child; Hippolyta was sorry for this assault on her blissful innocence. Childhood must be left behind, but not yet.

Please, not yet.

"And war ravaged the earth," Hippolyta said.

Ares was our enemy. That's why our tradition is to train constantly, because that's how we beat him. And if he ever came back, we'd beat him again, Diana recited to herself, as she tiptoed from her bedchamber once again, sneaking past her guards and a strolling peacock and slipping into the stone chamber where Antiope waited for her. It had been a week now, and her mother didn't suspect a thing. She felt a tiny flicker of guilt, but it was dwarfed by the joy of learning how to fight. What had Aunt Antiope said? A scorpion had to sting, a wolf to hunt... and a little girl to grow up.

This time Antiope had brought swords. She put Diana through her paces, making a thrust, watching closely as Diana mimicked her action. Nodding. Moving on to the next thrust. Then a parry. A slow-motion battle. *I'm going to save everybody.*

Little princess, big dreams.

Each night, Diana trained with Antiope. And each evening, Diana's mother continued the story of Ares.

"So the Gods created *us,* the Amazons, to influence man's heart with love and restore peace to the earth."

Greek warriors, men, and women looked on as Diana's mother Hippolyta, and Antiope, Eliana, Artemis, Phillipus, and all the other Amazons rose out of the sea, full-grown. The Greeks were awestruck by the majesty of her mother and all her perfect, strong, loving subjects. The bringers not of war, but of harmony.

"For a brief time, there *was* peace, even a unity among us all in the world," Hippolyta said.

"But it did not last," Antiope told Diana, taking up the story at their next training session. Sharing a breather—and, in truth, Diana was a bit sore and tired—they had built a campfire together, and Diana stared into the flames as Antiope described how Ares' army of men took up arms against the Amazons. He knew that they stood between him and the endless war he had promised to inspire in Zeus's human children, and he was determined to take the Amazons out of the equation.

Of course, since she was Queen, Ares had singled out Hippolyta—her brave mother taking on an army of men! Hippolyta had fought well, but under Ares's influence, the human warriors overpowered the Amazons and put them in chains. As Antiope spoke, Diana could see the followers of the God of War dragging her mother and all the Amazons out of a burning city. Her captive mother marched in the lead, head held high.

"Your mother, the Amazon Queen, led a revolt that freed us all from enslavement," Antiope said, describing the action—Hippolyta swinging her sword, a wild cheetah lunging and biting beside her. Diana had never seen her mother in her war-queen role, and her heart quickened at the thought.

"When Zeus led the Gods to our defense, Ares killed them, one by one," Antiope said, "until only Zeus himself remained."

Then in the story, Hippolyta broke the chains between her bracelets. It took Diana a minute to realize what Antiope was telling her: That Ares had killed all the gods, but in the end, he had not defeated the Amazons.

The Amazons are the only force on Earth that could stand up to him. Pride welled inside Diana. *And if anyone tries to attack the human beings again, we'll protect them, just like we did before.*

She asked her mother to tell the story over and over again, listening, pondering, etching it on her heart:

"While Zeus used the last of his power to stop Ares…"

Back in her bedchamber, Diana pictured the two Gods fighting and clashing in the eye of a massive storm, each at the edge of death. Zeus threw a thunderbolt—his last—hitting Ares.

" …striking him with such a blow, the God of War was forced to retreat. But Zeus knew Ares might one day return to finish his mission—an endless war where mankind will finally destroy themselves and us with them."

Ares was swallowed up by darkness next, and Diana darted a glance at the shadows in the room. She imagined the courage it had required for the Amazons to take on a God, the sheer strength they had garnered to defeat him. *I want to be an Amazon like that.* But she was not. *Not yet.*

Zeus had created a retreat for the Amazons, a heaven on Earth. Curls of stone and mountainous towers rose into the mists as valleys plunged toward a cerulean sea. Waterfalls both gentle and mighty tumbled into grottos of stalactites and artesian pools and splashed land bridges dotted with flowers; clear streams burbled through lush green fields and cliffs from which sprang homes and meeting halls hewn from golden rock and whitest marble. Sheltered bowls of land had been formed into arenas and the amphitheater where plays and poetry festivals were held. Pines towered; tiny birds nested. Gentle ocean waves lapped the beaches. Curling vines and feathered ferns softened the soaring columns of stone, the large council chamber, and the warlike appearance of the military garrisons. She saw it all with new eyes—the eyes of a protective warrior cherishing her homeland and vowing to keep each precious blade of grass, each grain of sand, as pristine and untouched as it was at this moment.

As if to underscore her oath, at their next training session, she got in a few extra-powerful licks with her sword—to her aunt's surprise and satisfaction.

"But in the event that he did," Antiope said, picking up the thread of the story at Diana's urging, "Zeus left us a weapon, one powerful enough to *kill* a God. To destroy Ares before he could destroy mankind and us… with an endless war."

An endless war. It was a difficult thing to imagine, a war without end. In truth, for Diana, it was hard to imagine a war at all.

But at night, with soothing words, her mother attempted to quiet her restive mind: "With Zeus's dying breath, he created this island to shield us from the outside world. Somewhere Ares could not find us. And all has been quiet ever since."

Because of us, Diana thought, as she drifted off to sleep.

One morning, after breaking their fast with meat, figs, olives, and barley bread dipped in honey, mother and daughter mounted horses and surveyed Hippolyta's domain. The day was warm, the sky bright and clear as it met the deep blue water. The Queen often rode the hills and valleys of Themyscira so that all could see her and know that she was there to protect and defend them.

Together they gazed out to sea and Diana tried to

imagine what it had been like for the Amazons to rise from the waves fully formed. Her mother had never been a little girl. She had known everything forever. She didn't know what it was like to have to learn things. At least, that was what Diana guessed. The stories of Ares and his wars filled her with endless questions as she tried to comprehend a struggle she had never known, a foe she had never seen. All these years later, Mnemosyne's seeming obsession with Greeks and Spartans made sense.

"We give thanks to the Gods for this paradise," Hippolyta said, oblivious of the churnings of her daughter's inquisitive mind as she raised her open palms to the memory of Mt. Olympus.

"And the Godkiller?" Diana asked, unable to keep from seizing this thinnest of openings into the subject. They had given thanks to the Gods for the Godkiller, too. She was sure Antiope had told her that.

For a moment, Hippolyta drew back, her lips parting in surprise. She said carefully, "The Godkiller?"

"Yes," Diana said. "The weapon that is strong enough to kill a God. Can I see it, Mother?"

A strange expression washed over her mother's face. She studied Diana hard; then her mouth curled downward as if she were sad. Something seemed to go out of her—that she was not so much making a choice as admitting some kind of defeat.

Together mother and daughter rode their mounts up Themyscira's tallest hillside, heading towards the stone keep on its peak. The armory was a high tower that seemed to morph from a mountain into a building, as did many of the curving buildings on the vast island. A single window like a God's eye overlooked both land and surrounding sea. Diana held her reins taut in eagerness.

Behind them rode the queen's guards, horse tack jingling, leather creaking. They stopped their horses at the courtyard at the foot of the tower and dismounted onto the flagging.

The armory gate was made of heavy iron, spiked with spearheads, and locked from the outside. Diana stuck her face between the bars. Inside it was very dark and smelled of damp and the sea. The chief guard unlocked the gate and entered before them, lighting a series of torches along the walls as she went. Diana followed her mother down the bleak tunnel. Ahead there was a rectangle of light. It got brighter and brighter as they neared it.

They stepped from the tunnel into an open-air courtyard.

"The Gods gave us many gifts. One day you'll know them all. This is where we keep them," Hippolyta told her.

In the center of the courtyard, protected by spirals of curving metal, an ornately crafted sword gleamed. The double-dragon hilt and ancient runes etched into the blade caught the light. She reached out and reverently touched it. In this moment, she felt as if Zeus's hand lay in hers.

"The Godkiller," she said in awe. "It's beautiful."

Hippolyta watched her carefully.

"Who would wield it?" Diana asked.

"I pray it will never be called to arms. But only the fiercest among us ever could… and that is not you, Diana."

With that, the queen reached out, took hold of Diana's wrist, and pulled her hand away from the sword. Diana was abashed.

"So you see, you are safe. And there is nothing for you to concern yourself with."

But it was everything Diana wanted to concern herself with. She knew what she felt inside when she saw the others fight. How it made her heart pound to realize that she could do it too. With this weapon in her hand …

Someday I will show you what I can do, she thought.

But one look from her mother told Diana that today was not that day.

3

After seven mortal years of secret training, Diana had made considerable gains. Not only had she grown in size and strength, but she had begun to be able to anticipate Antiope's intentions from her stance, her repertoire of moves, and what the general perceived as her own personal strengths. Diana couldn't always put this understanding to use, and there was still frustration when she wasn't quite quick enough to take advantage or when her footwork still required effort.

Case in point: the two of them were in the middle of a training session among the pines, swords clanging, sparks flying. Antiope was on the attack, hammering with forehand and backhand slashes. Diana could not spin away; she could only retreat, shielding herself from the blows by meeting the general's sword with her own.

"You keep doubting yourself, Diana," Antiope growled as she drove Diana back, step after step.

"No, I don't," Diana said defiantly, grunting out each syllable as she parried the rain of blows.

"Yes, you do," Antiope countered.

"No, I don't," Diana insisted.

Antiope pressed even harder, doubling the number of strikes, forcing Diana to stumble as she retreated. Her legs tangled under her and she went down hard on her backside.

"But you must dig deeper or you will never find your inner power," Antiope said. "You're stronger than you believe…"

"Diana!" a voice cried.

Heart pounding, Diana scrambled to her feet as Hippolyta rode toward her with her retinue of guards in tow. *Oh, no, we've finally been caught.* Diana had thought their secret would be safe forever. She and Antiope had always been so careful.

The Queen climbed down from her saddle, furious. "Are you hurt?"

"Mother, I'm fine," Diana said. "I was just…"

"Training," Hippolyta finished for her. Her mother turned to Antiope and said, "It seems I am not the revered Queen I should be. Disobeyed, betrayed by my own sister…"

"No, Mother," Diana interrupted. "It was me. I asked her to…"

The Queen nodded at her guards. "Take her to the palace," she said. Then, less sternly, "Off you go."

Crestfallen, Diana allowed herself to be led away, remembering a time long ago when she had ridden on her mother's saddle to be deposited back in her schoolroom. As she passed by her aunt, the two locked gazes. Antiope silently reassured her, but in truth, Antiope wasn't her usual confident self.

* * *

"You left me no choice, Hippolyta," the general said when her niece had been taken out of earshot. "You neglect your duty if she cannot fight."

"You speak of a time that may never come," the Queen countered. "He may never return. He could have died of his wounds."

Antiope's eyes flashed. "Ares is still alive. You feel it as I do—in your bones. He is out there. And it's only a matter of time before he returns."

"The stronger she gets..." Hippolyta began, and Antiope saw the real fear in her eyes. Antiope softened, no longer worried for herself. The Queen wasn't truly angry. She was afraid.

"Hippolyta, I love her as you do. But this is the only way to truly protect her."

The Queen looked away for a moment. Antiope knew how to read her sister. It was clear that her words had had an effect, and that Hippolyta was terribly torn. Diana was a member of the royal family, and no fiercer warriors dwelled on Themyscira. To be the only one who didn't know how to fight—no matter the reason—was humiliating to the princess, at the very least. And at the worst? Highly dangerous. Antiope prepared to say all this to her sister.

Hippolyta stayed silent. Then the Queen turned to Antiope, resolved. "You will train her harder than every Amazon before her," she ground out. Emotion ran deep through her words.

"Hippolyta..." *Do not worry. Do not fear,* Antiope wanted to tell her. This was hard for her sister, very hard.

"Five times harder—ten times harder until she is better than even you." Antiope nodded and would have spoken, but Hippolyta continued. "She must never know the truth about what she is and how she came to be."

Antiope dipped her head, sealing a wordless vow. They were of one mind again. The sisters both loved Diana, and they both wanted what was best for her. They both knew that she was unaware of her true heritage.

And they both prayed she would never have cause to find out what it was.

Years passed.

The training grounds echoed with the sounds of combat. The Amazons were out in full force, reveling in their ferocious strength. At one end of the field, a striking young woman with braided dark hair ran at full speed, did a perfect shoulder roll, and came onto her feet with bow drawn, arrow loaded and nocked. The bowstring released and with a sizzling sound the arrow flew halfway across the expanse, high over the heads of the other fighters, arcing up into the blue sky until it vanished, then reappearing as it fell—a rainbow that ended dead center on the painted straw target being dragged at a gallop.

Diana, Princess of Themyscira, glanced up to the hillside, where her mother observed on horseback with her cortège.

Diana drew her sword. Ahead a gauntlet of Amazons awaited her. Her skin already glazed with perspiration, she immediately attacked in a frenzy, sword flashing in the sun. With each one down, another came at her. She deflected heavy blows, absorbing them until her assailant ran out of steam. Her current opponent pressed against her, their blades locked at the handgrips, straining practically nose to nose. For an instant, neither could gain ground.

Over the woman's shoulder, Diana saw Artemis crossing the field at a trot, carrying an axe, eager to join in the fight against her. Suddenly the prospect of two Amazons at once loomed and the idea thrilled her. Seeing that help was on the way out of the corner of her eye, her opponent relaxed. That was all it took. Diana spun out of the deadlock, turning her back on the flatfooted adversary just long enough to coil into a wind up. She smashed the metal arm guard of her sword hand against the side of the Amazon's helmet, which went flying. The clang of the blow resounded across the field and the Amazon's knees buckled. Diana saw her eyes roll back in her head. As the defeated warrior hit the ground face first, limp but most definitely only stunned, Diana was ready to meet the onrushing Artemis.

Her teeth bared, the Amazon's most accomplished brawler attacked with an overhand slash of the axe that Diana blocked with her sword. The sheer power of the impact sent electric tingles down the backs of both legs, but her knees held. She easily caught the next backhanded blow, which seemed to come at half speed, as if her opponent was slicing through heavy syrup. Artemis clearly couldn't produce the same momentum standing still.

Letting the next swing whoosh past, Diana slammed hard into Artemis's elbow, making her wince and stagger away. For a second she seemed to lose her grip on the axe handle, then caught it. The older woman's eyes widened as Diana circled away, smiling. If Artemis wanted to keep her status as the strongest warrior, she had a fight on her hands.

Once again, everything slowed down for Diana. Without looking down, she could sense the other woman's points of balance, the relative weight on either foot, the tension in her legs. The positioning of her arms and weapon reduced the number of possible attack strategies to a handful. And when Artemis made her move to resume the attack, those possibilities dwindled even further.

The all-out charge, the sharp crash of metal on metal, then the quick drop for a leg sweep—Diana knew what she was going to do at the same moment she did. The leg sweep cut through empty air as Diana pressed down and jumped, drawing her knees up to her chest. Then she simply rolled off Artemis's shield, landing on the balls of her feet facing her opponent. Artemis slammed the side of the axe against Diana's head. Dizziness rushed through her, but she tamped it down.

Others watched in respectful silence as Artemis feigned another attack, lunging with raised axe only to stop short, obviously trying to figure out Diana's instinctive reaction.

But there was none. Diana knew the rush was a fake because she could read the tension in Artemis's body— she was holding back.

They began to circle one another, weapons lowered, bodies taut and predatory, like lionesses. Daring each other to begin the fight. Something had to break.

Diana was ready for it when it did.

Instead of a straightforward attack, Artemis chose a flashier approach, with 360-degree spins and axe slashes coming from all angles. Diana answered every attack and prepared for a full-on assault. It came, and at the end,

Artemis's axe fell to the ground as Diana disarmed her. Diana pointed her sword at her and Artemis lowered her head in submission. She had been bested.

But Diana's trials were not over. Now Antiope came at her from the right side with drawn sword. There was no time to think, only to react.

It was absolutely wonderful.

Sparks flew from the edges of their blades as Diana met the attack with measured strikes of her own. The intensity of her teacher's assault surprised her. For the first time in all their years of training, Antiope was committed to sheer domination. They circled each other in a predatory dance, parrying each other's thrusts. One mistake, a slip, could mean serious injury. A blunt sword edge could still split a skull or break an arm.

"Harder, Diana!" Antiope growled, lunging at her. "You're stronger than this. Again!"

And Diana answered; she found a deep well and inside it, the steady thrumming of her own heart. It was a warrior's heart—the very core of her essence. The flow of combat slowed to a crawl, and her sword seemed to weigh nothing, the very force of gravity weakened.

She moved with a speed and with power that clearly surprised Antiope, even though she'd asked for it. Diana drove her teacher backward with a blinding series of forehands and backhands. And the power behind the blows made Antiope grimace. Again and again the sword strikes rained down. Diana hammered the hand guard of her sword so hard that the weapon flew out of Antiope's hand and cartwheeled through the air. Standing tall, she pointed the tip of her sword at the general, who raised her hands in surrender. Lowering her weapon, Diana turned to her mother, eyes beaming, anticipating the approval that was certainly now her due.

Out of nowhere a crushing blow struck her in the temple and sent her flying. Weaving, she swayed on her armor-shod feet, fighting to keep balance as stars burst behind her eyelids.

Then Antiope attacked again. "Never let your guard down," she said. "You expect a battle to be fair. A battle will never be fair."

Antiope hacked and slashed at her. The general knocked Diana's sword out of her fingers. Diana staggered backwards, then fell to her knees and crossed her arms protectively over her chest to block the blows of the onslaught, her bracelets clanging together.

Boooooossshhhh!

They sizzled; then, like a secret door opened in the center of her being, a field of pure energy blasted forth. The air rippled and shone. The impact of the force knocked Antiope off her feet and made Diana stumble backwards. For a second, it was like looking at the world through a golden lens, and then the image faded.

On the cliff top, Hippolyta's world changed forever. Her eyes wide, her heart seizing, she murmured to herself, "What have I done?"

In the field, Diana stared at her bracelets, the release of unthinkable power. What had just happened? The assembled crowd stood frozen by what they had just seen; no one spoke. She wanted to tell them how incredible it had felt—the raw power, the thrill of it. She opened her mouth—

"What have you done?" Hippolyta cried, breaking the silence.

Diane looked to Antiope and saw blood streaming from a cut on her forehead as an Amazon attended her. The general looked dazed. Stunned and amazed, Diana started to back away.

"Wait, Diana. Wait," Antiope said, in an attempt to calm her.

"I'm sorry," Diana said. She was amazed. And excited. What had just happened? She took a step toward her aunt. Antiope held up a hand as if to wave her off.

Diana looked around. Everyone was staring at her. She turned to her mother and saw tension in her face.

Fear of her?

No, Mother. This is power. Amazon power, she wanted to tell her. *This is something incredible—for us.*

Diana backed away, then dashed up a grassy embankment. She ran to the edge of a cliff overlooking the sea. The winds gusted around her as she stared at her open palms. What secret had she unlocked? What door had she opened? She closed her eyes and lifted her face to the sky as deep within her, she sensed a vibrant strength, something new. It was as if she had completed an altogether different rite of initiation than what had played out on the training field. She opened her hands and studied them. Where had that power come from?

Then she heard another strange sound—a sawing buzz that grew louder and softer as if it, too, was buffeted by the sea wind. As she peered upward, the sky itself seemed to bubble and shimmer—and then a large object manifested as if out of thin air. It had a pair of wings like a gigantic bird. A tawny yellow bird. It was flying erratically, dipping up and down, veering from side to side, and smoke trailed from its tail.

As the object began to angle in a sickening dive towards the water, she saw what looked like a human figure restrained inside it. Before the person could get clear, the object crashed into the sea, throwing up a plume of white foam.

Without a second of hesitation, Diana bounded upward off the cliff, arched into the sky, and knifed through hundreds of feet of empty air. She splashed neatly into the waves, propelling herself through the ocean depths as object and passenger sank rapidly toward the bottom.

I'm outgunned and outrun, the pilot thought, tugging at his shoulder strap. It would not release. *At least I caused some damage before I died.*

When he couldn't jump clear before impact, he sank back into the cockpit, grabbed the joystick, and braced himself. The downward view of the sea over the side of the machine gun tilted madly as his air speed spiked. The German Fokker Eindecker fuselage was made of sheet metal, stronger than the coated linen of the British fighter planes, but no plane was designed to absorb a nosedive crash.

At the very last second he pulled back on the stick with both gloved hands. As the nose struggled to rise, g-forces slammed him into the seat, the monoplane fuselage vibrated violently, and even before he hit the water, the sheet metal rivets began popping out—it sounded like small-caliber gunfire.

On impact he was slammed forward and lost consciousness for a second. The cold water pouring into the cockpit woke him with a start. Looking to either side, he realized the plane was sinking with him in it. He pushed down on the release catch of the seat restraint again. It was still jammed. Behind him there was a shrill creak, then another. When he looked back he saw a deep fissure in the metal near the tail widening, then the tail broke free of the fuselage. Its flotation was the only thing keeping the plane above water. With the engine as an anchor, the nose, then the wings of the ruined aircraft slipped under the surface. He managed to suck down a deep breath of air an instant before he sank into the depths. Light above him grew dimmer and dimmer.

But I'm not done yet, he thought. *I've got to get to London.*

Through the haze of ocean, oxygen-starved, he looked up in frustration at the surface. Even as he fought to hold his breath, the dark and the cold closed in on him. As his eyes fluttered shut he felt a sudden rush of warmth. He opened them again. A woman was staring right at him, practically nose to nose.

An angel come to take me home.

In the water, grabbing hold of the padded edge of the opening where the human occupant was trapped, Diana pulled herself closer as the wreck was sucked down. She couldn't tell if the person was alive or dead. The eyes were closed. Though great bubbles were escaping from inside the contraption, no air came from the nose or mouth. Reaching way into the opening, she took hold of an armpit, and bracing her legs against the side of the thing, ripped free. The wreckage continued to sink, disappearing beneath her as she kicked, pulling the limp body to the surface. A bag of some kind trailed behind.

As they bobbed in the sunlight one thing was certain: it wasn't an Amazon she had saved. The person was wearing a full body suit of heavy material with a fur collar and long gloves. Adjusting her grip, she rolled onto her back and began towing the unresisting body towards the shoreline.

4

Capture the pilot at all costs.

That was the order from Command. Four wooden launches had been deployed from the *Schwaben,* the battleship sent to track the plane to... where? It seemed to have disappeared into thin air.

The German soldier riding in the bow of the first boat squinted ahead but could see nothing except fog and water. The sputtering buzz of the plane had become their only beacon. He glanced back at the other soldiers hunched on the boat's bench seats, lanterns up, with heads lowered.

Then the tone of the buzz changed; the sputtering grew worse. The soldier heard a faint whine. Growing louder. Then a *whomp* as it hit the water. The plane had crashed! Perhaps two hundred feet directly in front of them, but maybe closer—the fog played tricks with sound.

The soldiers in the boat let out a cheer. The tillerman gunned the boat's motor, maintaining course. They had to reach the aircraft before it sank and all was lost. The other following behind sped up too, keeping each other well in sight.

Leaning out over the bow, the soldier strained to see some sign of the wreck. He reached over the side to touch the tail and his hand disappeared into something that wasn't fog, more like a glittering smoke. When he jerked his hand away, just for a second he got a glimpse of something ahead, as if a curtain had been ripped away—a beautiful island with tall trees, cliffs, and a broad beach. Then the fog closed in and it was gone.

He shook his head to clear it. No such island existed; there was nothing but open sea for hundreds of miles. Perhaps his overtaxed eyes were playing tricks on him? He looked back at the tillerman, who apparently hadn't seen anything.

Summoning his courage, he leaned out again, much farther this time, and again the fog vanished and the island reappeared, bathed in warm sunlight. Farther to his right, about a quarter mile between the boat and the island, he saw something in the water. Two heads moving together. Someone swimming. Someone was towing the pilot to the beach.

Stunned, he drew back to the bow. And as he did, once again the cold, wet fog enveloped him. He turned to the stern and waved at the tillerman, pointing off into the impenetrable wall of mist.

"The pilot! He's there!"

The tillerman gave him a dubious look, but slowly turned the boat in the direction he indicated. The rumble of the battle cruiser grew louder as it crept up behind them.

Aboard the battle cruiser, the captain raised his field glasses. He blinked at an island that shouldn't have been there, an island not noted on any chart. On the beach dead ahead of them, one person was dragging another out of the water. The person being dragged was dressed in a flight suit. It had to be their quarry. The rescuer was a young woman in a scanty costume. It was all so strange—

—But orders were orders, and they had to capture that man.

Without lowering his binoculars he hand-signaled the lieutenant to make speed. They would make a full assault on that beachhead—

—He blinked—

—The beachhead that kept disappearing.

5

Diana swam for shore with the limp body in tow. She couldn't tell if the person she had rescued was alive or dead. She timed their crossing of the outside of the reef with an incoming wave that lifted them up and over. Inside the barrier of rock and coral, the water was calmer and she quickly reached the shallows.

Then she dragged the body by the arms onto the sand. She realized she was not only pulling a body in a heavy one-piece suit, but a bag on a strap over the shoulder. When she let go of the arms, she stared down at the face. Stared hard at sharp angles, a strong jawline, stubble on the cheeks and chin. Her breath caught. This was a man. Here, on the protected beach of her hidden homeland.

Wonder; warmth, an echo of power as she gazed down on him—the first man she had ever seen in person. He looked like the best of the warriors she had studied in her mother's triptych. A personification of man's goodness.

But was he dead? His eyes were closed, his lips slack.

She was moved, hoping she'd gotten to him in time. Tentatively she reached out to touch his cheek.

The man jerked awake, squinting into the sun. As she withdrew her hand, he blinked and looked up at her. They locked gazes, and he blinked as if startled. Then he simply stared at her.

"Wow," he said. His eyes were blue. So blue.

She laughed with the pleasure of …what, discovery? Something more than that. "You are a… man."

"Yes, I mean…" He paused, and when he continued his voice was suddenly even deeper. "Yeah. Do I not look like a… Where am I?"

"You are on Themyscira. Who are you?"

"I'm one of the good guys," the man said. He gestured. "And those are the bad guys."

Four small boats brimming with men were speeding for the beach.

"You know," the man continued, "Germans."

"Germans?"

"We gotta get out of here." He stripped off the sodden outer suit, revealing a gray uniform.

"Diana!"

Her mother and her guard lined the bluff overlooking the beach. Bows were drawn and arrows aimed at the rescued man beside her. Diana had no doubt that they could miss her and hit him.

"Step away from her! Now!" Hippolyta commanded. To her troops, "Ready your bows!"

The man's eyes widened. "They have guns, right?"

Diana just stared at him. She didn't understand what he was talking about. Behind them, the small boats were in the shallows preparing to land on the beach.

"Fire!" Hippolyta commanded.

Another wave of mounted guards swept up behind the Queen. They whipped out their bows, and as they notched their arrows, an Amazon on foot ran down the line, lighting the arrowheads with a torch. They flexed their bows, aiming higher, to rain arrows down on the invading craft.

Flaming arrows whooshed from the cliff top, sailed high over Diana's head, and pin-cushioned the four small boats. Most found targets. Men in gray uniforms staggered and fell. The barking clatter from their weapons shocked Diana. Tiny objects zipped past her and the man she had saved like angry bees, throwing up puffs of dry sand and sparking chips out of the rock formation beyond them.

"Get down!" the man cried as he grabbed hold of Diana and swung her down behind the nearest available cover, a boulder outcrop. This put them both out of the line of fire as the men in gray uniforms splashed out of the surf, fanning out onto the beach.

More Amazons joined the ranks of those stationed along the edge of the cliff, thundering to join their sisters. They were led by the athletic daredevil Orana. As Diana watched, a wave of warriors filled grappling arrows with lines attached across the curved beach and into the rocks and sand. They flung themselves down, firing arrow after arrow at the invaders the man had labeled Germans with deadly accuracy. Orana threw herself—literally—into the fray.

Movement out of the corner of her eye made Diana whirl to her right. A German soldier had flanked them; his weapon was up and aimed. The next second, he fired. There was a *crack;* a flash and puff of smoke burst from the end of the weapon. Plowing through both, a projectile left the barrel, heading straight for Diana's head. Instantly, the unnerving sensation of time slowing down reasserted itself. The track of the little object as it crawled through the air towards her was mesmerizing.

The man she had saved tackled her from the side, driving her to the sand, and the projectile missed her.

She looked over her shoulder and saw the object sailing in a perfect straight line towards Orana, who dangled on the grappling line, pulling another arrow from the quiver on her back, eyes searching out her next shot. Diana screamed a warning, but Orana didn't hear her. She was so focused on the battle; she didn't know what was coming—

The projectile slammed into Orana's chest, smashing her hard against the cliff wall. She shuddered from the shockwave, head to foot, then collapsed. The bow and arrow dropped from her hands and she hung there, head and arms drooping, swinging against the cliff face.

"No!" Diana screamed. Orana did not rouse. She dangled from the line, slack. Orana was immortal. She could not die.

But we can be killed. But she couldn't believe it. She could not believe it.

"Keep your head down!" the man warned her.

And then Diana was back in the battle and the need to defend her people. Taking up prone and kneeling positions in the sand, the Germans rained gunfire on the cliff. The noise was deafening. Though shields were up, the projectiles still somehow found their mark, and cut through the defenders like a scythe. Amazons were struck and they crumpled from their saddles, falling off the cliff and toppling to the beach below. This was not the kind of battle Diana had trained for. What manner of combat was this? Impersonal. Inhuman. Indiscriminate.

The German who had killed Orana turned his weapon towards the cliff. Before he could shoot again an arrow hit his gun, filling the barrel with point and shaft, rendering it useless. But he was either already in the act of firing, or the shock of the arrow strike made him flinch; the gun went off anyway. Something had to give, and it did—spectacularly. With an ear-splitting crack the end of the weapon blew apart, sending pieces of hot metal flying in all directions, but mostly back at the shooter. The soldier's helmet blew off and he fell to his back, clutching his face.

At that moment a stampede of Amazons on horseback charged through the massive stone archway that led to the beach. *My sister warriors!* Majestic and frenzied, they filled the gap, wall to wall, and, led by Antiope, burst through the roiling clouds of dust they had raised. With her younger sister, Menalippe, and Artemis at her side, the general deflected a flurry of bullets with her shield and rode down the nearest Germans before they could reload. With slashes of her sword she hacked through their ranks, leaving a trail of bodies. Amazons soared into the air, firing, twisting and turning and planting their landings back into the sand. They flung themselves sideways off their saddles, raining arrows and javelins on the invaders.

The blue-eyed man nudged Diana and pointed at a

soldier moving quick and low. The man was sneaking into position behind a nearby rock. "Stay there!" he ordered her.

She caught a glint of a knife in the blue-eyed man's hand. It had a long, narrow double-edged blade with a cross guard. A dirk designed for one thing and one thing only—killing other humans. He jumped over the top of the rock and leapt on the German, driving him down out of sight. A second later he reappeared holding the man's rifle. He turned toward the sea and began firing at the steady flow of Germans advancing from the water line.

Beyond, the enormous ship that had brought the Germans had hit the coral reefs. Black, gritty smoke from the sinking battleship swept across the reef and over the beach. It smelled like it had come from the burning pits of hell.

No longer able to contain herself, Diana grabbed up a bow and arrow, drew back the bowstring, and shot one of the Germans. She let more arrows fly. Then she hefted the sword of a fallen Amazon and rushed into the battle. She remembered what Antiope had said about not holding back and not trusting her adversaries to be honorable. And for the first time, Diana understood exactly what she meant.

When a German attacked in a mad bull rush, she deflected his bayonet with her shield, pivoted to let him rush past, and used her sword in a precise backhand stroke. The soldier squealed and crashed face first in the sand. He shouted at her in his native tongue and the others came at her two and three at a time. But the attacks were uncoordinated and the soft sand hampered their speed. They were so naturally lead-footed that she easily beat them back, and when one faltered in retreat, feet tangling, she used the pommel of the sword and a deft, powerful punch to the chin to drop him to the ground.

Frustration made the survivors more reckless. When one of them tried to shoulder and fire his gun at her, its length was a handicap. She moved in a blur, closing the gap before he could fire. The German screeched as he dropped the gun. Diana booted him in the chest and his head snapped back and he crumpled to the sand.

As Diana found her rhythm in the battle, Antiope's voice cut through the din. "Charge!"

They worked together, collaborating, a true tribe, taking every advantage they could as they learned the battle techniques of their adversaries. The Germans' weapons had to be reloaded with a bolt-like apparatus after each shot, which left them vulnerable to the fast-moving warriors. With no time to reload, the men used their bayonets against swords and spears.

The company of Amazons pressed forward, driving the invaders back towards the sea. The Germans waiting in the boats couldn't fire without hitting their own. The soldiers quickly discovered that a short blade on the end of a gun, no matter how sharp, was no match for thirty inches of tempered steel. Antiope and her cohort made good progress at first; unmoving Germans littered the beach in their wake. But the advance slowed as the remaining men in the boats hurried to join the fight. Some had very short guns that could be fired with one hand. Those weapons worked devastatingly well at close quarters. So well that Antiope stalled short of victory.

Then Hippolyta and her guard swept down onto the beach. The Queen slashed her way through the Germans, using knee pressure to guide her horse so she had both hands free to fight. Supremely confident, she pulled away from her cohort as she hurried to reinforce Antiope.

On foot, Antiope yanked the arrows from her quiver and planted them in the sand. She crouched beside them and strung her bow, arrow after arrow thinning the Germans' ranks. Hippolyta dismounted and joined her sister in battle. They fought close together, first defensively, but as the number of opponents dropped—literally falling to the sand—they began to advance in triumph.

"Shield!" Antiope shouted to Menalippe.

Diana had watched this maneuver many times on the practice field, but never in the heat of combat. Menalippe took her shield in both hands and held it parallel to the ground. The general ran at her, jumped onto the shield, and used it like a springboard to vault high in the air. Airborne, Antiope released three arrows, hitting three soldiers simultaneously, a fierce and graceful act.

One of the remaining soldiers turned and raised his gun to fire at her, but the man Diana had rescued fired first. The well-aimed shot struck just below the edge of the German's helmet, in front of his ear. The helmet was chin-strapped on so it didn't fly off, but the invader's head snapped to the side and his knees buckled, gun slipping from his hands.

The stranger had saved Antiope's life, Diana realized. She was only unfocused for a second, but it was long enough for another soldier to take aim at Diana.

"Diana!" the blue-eyed man shouted, swinging his sights onto the new target.

Before he could shoot, the German fired. Antiope was already in motion. Deliberately, she darted forward and took the bullet that had been intended for her niece.

"No!" Diana screamed. Not her aunt. Not her trainer, her confidante, her sister in arms. *No.*

The general's powerful body doubled over and twisted, then toppled to its side on the sand. As the German tried frantically to reload, ejecting a brass shell casing from the weapon, the man she had rescued fired. The soldier was bowled onto his back by the bullet's impact and his arms and legs went slack.

"Antiope!" Diana cried as she raced to her side. The reverberating noise of battle, the strewn bodies, all of it disappeared. There was only her fallen teacher and friend. Her aunt.

"No! Please no!" She reached out to cradle the general's head.

Antiope struggled to speak. Blood leaked from beneath her armor, pooling on the dry sand. There was blood on her pale lips. Her eyes were glazing over. "Diana... the time has come... you... you must..."

"What?" Diana fought back tears. So much blood. And agony. She could see it in Antiope's eyes. Amazons fought against showing weakness and pain. "What? Antiope!"

The general whispered, "Godkiller... Diana, go... Godkiller."

Diana leaned over her, face pressed close, willing her aunt to prevail in her fight for life. "Go where? Antiope!"

And then there was nothing in Antiope's eyes "No!"

The Queen rushed to Diana's side, falling to her knees beside the lifeless body. "Sister!" she cried in desperation.

But Antiope was beyond hearing. Diana sank back, incredulous, numb. The reality of her loss was almost too much to bear.

Hippolyta jumped to her feet, sword in hand, and turned on the rescued man in the gray uniform. "You!" she snarled, cocking back the blade as she charged, clearly intending to slice him in half.

Diana bolted from the sand and put herself between them. "Mother, no! He fought at my side against his own people."

"The man fights against his own people." Menalippe's voice dripped with contempt.

"They weren't my people," the man said. He had made no attempt to defend himself against the Queen; now he let the gun he held fall to the sand.

"Then why do you wear their colors?" Menalippe said.

"Tell us," Artemis demanded.

The man looked down at his uniform. "I can't tell you that."

Menalippe asked, "What is your name?"

"I can't tell you that, either."

"We should kill him right now and be done with it," Venelia said.

Phillipus interrupted the Queen's guard, her voice controlled despite the loss of her friend. "He dies and we know nothing about who they are and why they came."

One of the secrets to Phillipus's prowess on the battlefield was her ability to strategize; in the heated moment of victory dearly bought, the other Amazons paid heed.

A death sentence averted, or merely delayed?

Time would tell—but only if the man would give up his secrets.

6

The battle was over, and the Amazon survivors convened
in the throne room, a cavernous grotto of rock, bathed
by day in sunlight and at night by the moon. Twin circles,
two proud shields, flanked the spiral of Andromeda.
Golden stairs led to the dais where Hippolyta held
court, Diana one step below. There were injuries among
the warriors, some severe, but no one sat in the chairs.
Diana herself had been cut on the arm. Her heart hurt;
her head spun. No story of Ares's wrath had prepared
her for this day.

But as she must, Diana's mother, the Queen, put aside
her sorrows and focused on preventing further tragedy.
She called for the prisoner, and Diana could see that it
took every ounce of her restraint not to kill him then
and there. Instead, Hippolyta forced him to kneel on the
throne room's polished floor, her guard detail on high
alert, and threw the Lasso of Hestia around him. He was
bleeding from injuries he had sustained in the battle,
and bound around the chest and upper arms by the loop
of golden lasso that Menalippe controlled.

Diana raised her chin and watched as he struggled, his eyes clamped shut, his face in a frozen grimace. He didn't want to speak, but the glowing rope forced anyone captured within it to speak the truth. They must have the truth. She must.

"My name's Captain Steve Trevor," he said, gritting his teeth. "Pilot... American Expeditionary Force. Serial number 814192. That's all I'm at liberty to s..."

Captain Steve Trevor. Diana silently sounded out the name. "Captain" was a title; the Amazons used it as well. They had already known he was a warrior, but it was clear from the looks passed among the Queen, her government cabinet, and her highest-ranking warriors that they didn't know what a "pilot" or an "American Expeditionary Force" were. And as for the number, that was another unknown.

Diana studied the others' faces: the remnants of Hippolyta's guards, Antiope's warriors, and the Senators. They all showed strain in the aftermath of the attempted invasion. This man's fate had not yet been decided.

Steve Trevor continued, "Assigned... to British Intelligence." He looked down at the glowing rope. "What the hell is this thing anyway?"

"The Lasso of Hestia compels you to reveal the truth." Diana gazed down at him with authority.

"It is pointless—and painful—to resist," Menalippe added.

"What is your mission?" Hippolyta demanded.

"Whoever you are," he said, "you're in more danger than you think."

Menalippe tightened the Lasso, making him wince.

"What is your mission?" the Queen repeated.

"I'm a… spy," Steve Trevor said. "I'm a spy, a spy, a *spy*."

Snared by the golden rope, unable to resist, the truth came pouring out of him.

"I was working under cover for British Intelligence when they got word that the leader of the German Army, General Ludendorff, was visiting a secret military installation in the Ottoman Empire…"

Diana looked to her mother for translation, but her face was blank.

"I posed as one of their pilots, then flew in with them."

I have no idea how to shut myself up, Steve thought as he described a massive hangar-like complex in Turkey heavily guarded by German soldiers.

"According to our intel," he told the Amazons, "the Germans had no troops left, no money, no munitions of any kind…"

What he found when he infiltrated his target area was something quite different. The building was an immense, highly sophisticated munitions factory with assembly line conveyor belts, furnaces to forge the casings for explosives, milling machinery, presses to load the warheads into their metal shells. Heat, oil, dust, filings. The bubbling of molten metal, the acrid stench of shellac. The roof was glass, presumably to let in more natural light, and it was manned by silent, elderly men, and by sullen, frightened women and children, hundreds of them. They moved with the trembling, dizzy gait of the starved and sleep deprived. Slave laborers, either taken from the local population or imported from elsewhere in Turkey, conscripted for the mass production of weapons of war.

The flopsweat of fear. The scent of death.

"But our intel was wrong. The Germans had the Turks building bombs for them. And not just bombs…"

Contained within the bomb factory was a scientific laboratory, and nested inside that, a forbidding-looking testing chamber. Through a window, Steve saw General Ludendorff approach a slight figure who was dressed in head-to-toe protective gear inside the lab—a dark green smock and rubber gloves that came up to the elbows. When the mask and goggles came off Steve saw who it was. Pay dirt.

She quickly scribbled something in a green notebook then, exuding confidence, greeted the general with respect and apparent pleasure. Ludendorff was brisk, but obviously eager to see her newest development. He was a war monger who lived for the battle. Combat was his staff of life—it sustained him, fed him. He relished any field advantage as some cherished jewels, or gold, or even loved ones. He reserved his love for one thing and one thing only: total world domination, to be won by the armies under his personal command.

"New weapons," Steve continued his story for the Amazons. "Secret weapons invented by Ludendorff's chief psychopath, Dr. Isabel Maru."

When the scientist turned her head, his stomach clenched. Flesh-colored metal plates covered the lower half of her nose, two-thirds of her mouth on the right side, and three-fourths of her chin, hiding the damage previous failed experiments had done to her. Even though he had been briefed about the extent of the prosthesis, the effect startled him.

"Boys in the trenches call her 'Dr. Poison.' For good reason,'" he told the Amazons, wondering if they understood what he was talking about. Where were the men? He had yet to see a single one. Had the Germans landed here before and murdered them? Why didn't these women have real weapons?

The woman holding onto the lasso gave it a tug. A sensation like heated electric shocks zinged through him. He continued his story.

He watched from the window as Dr. Maru led the general to her personal laboratory, to stand before the fully enclosed test chamber with a viewing window of heavy glass rimmed with a black gasket. Presumably airtight. There were dials and levers below the window.

Inside the test chamber sat a prisoner, his terrified face covered by what looked like a regulation British gas mask—rubber on the sides, chin, and forehead, round mouthpiece filter unit, two glass lenses for the eyes, and straps to hold it in place. His wrists and ankles were cuffed and restrained by chains. The top of the gas mask had a metal ring in it, and the ring was connected to another, smaller diameter chain that led up into the ceiling. Knowing Maru's background in chemical weapons, it wasn't difficult to guess what might be in store for the poor soul behind the glass.

In hushed tones Maru began to explain the experiment and chemical formulas to Ludendorff, but Steve was too far away to catch any of the details. They seemed to be quite chummy, heads almost touching as they reviewed her notebook.

Steve fought the urge to push closer so he could eavesdrop. One thing was certain: the general would not have traveled so far from the Fatherland without good reason. Clearly something momentous—and, knowing the doctor's history, horrendous—was about to be revealed. The prisoner in the chamber was an innocent pawn whom Steve could not protect.

As soon as Maru closed her notebook and set it down on the desk, she turned away. Steve realized that he could probably snake his hand through the half-open door and take it. He had to time his attempt perfectly; too soon and she would realize it was gone. Too late—

Steve inched closer.

Smiling with half her face, she opened a valve below the window, and a glowing gas began to flow into the sealed chamber. Inside the gas mask, the prisoner's eyes grew wide. His muffled screams for help could be heard through his mask, through the glass window.

Ludendorff watched the proceedings intently, occasionally turning his head to mutter something to his second in command. The gas filled the chamber and as Steve looked on, the mask on the subject began to disintegrate. Thin cracks appeared in the glass lenses, the canvas straps began to fray and discolor, and the metal parts around the mouthpiece looked like they were corroding. It was difficult to see, with the chamber filling with smoke.

Closer.

The doctor leered at the man in the mask, her face pressing closer to the pane, eyes urging on the outcome she desired—like she was cheering on a horse in a race.

But the process didn't escalate. There was no finish line, no winner.

The prisoner seemed to relax as the gas mask continued to protect him. His body language said he thought he was going to survive.

Dr. Maru whirled away from the glass. Her expression, or the half that was visible outside the metal plates, shifted from joy and triumph to doubt and anger.

Ludendorff let out a huff, shook back the cuff of his officer's great coat, peeled back the hem of a leather glove to check his wristwatch. The message was clear: you are wasting my time.

Instead of apologizing or explaining, an infuriated Dr. Maru reached out and pulled a lever beside the valve. Something whirred in the ceiling, and the chain connected to the top of the gas mask tightened. Before the prisoner could react, the mask was ripped from his face.

Steve heard his shrieks—

"From what I saw," Steve said with the lasso around his chest, "if Dr. Maru was able to complete her work, millions would die. The war would never end—I had to do something… dammit."

"I need more time," Maru told the general.

"Unfortunately, doctor, we do not have more time."

Everything Steve needed was in the green notebook, everything the Brits and their allies wanted to know. He had to chance it now. Coolly, he grabbed the notebook, turned, and walked briskly and calmly away.

"This work," Maru said. "This—"And that was when she noticed that the book was gone. "Stop him!"

Behind Steve there were angry shouts and the tramp of heavy boots. He burst out of the factory and raced through the courtyard, making for the crude Turkish airstrip. One of the fleet of Fokkers was idling, prop whirring, a pilot about to board.

Pops of pistol fire erupted from behind him. Bullets sailed over his head and wildly to his left and right. He ducked under the wing and slid, grabbing the pilot and yanking him out of his way.

He climbed into the single-seat cockpit as the plane as the Germans rushed in. Advancing the engine's throttle and working the foot pedals, he cut a hard left turn. Bullets struck the plane, punching holes in the sheet metal skin. No time for goggles or cap.

More bullets, dangerously close.

The Eindecker roared into the head wind. The added lift made his takeoff quick and easy. He pulled back on the stick and the plane responded, streaking up into the sky.

More gunfire rattled up from below, rifles this time. Bullets struck the side of the fuselage as he made a tight loop, swinging back over the installation and the airfield. He had what he wanted. It was a long way to Whitehall. The last thing he needed was aerial pursuit by a squadron of fighter planes. Diving toward the field, he steered with one hand and reached for the cockpit lever that fired the mounted Spandau IMG 08 machine gun. As he bore down on the row of parked planes, he pulled the trigger. Synched with the propeller, the machine gun appeared to fire right through the spinning blade. A line of 7.92 mm bullets stitched along the ground and through the aircraft, kicking up a flurry of dust. The aircraft exploded in flames, sending the German troops scattering for cover. He eased off. Spent shell casings fell through a hole and emptied into the fuselage.

Steve released the trigger, opened the throttle, and pulled back on the stick. He made another figure eight, and as the installation once again came into view, he saw two figures running for a parked command car. There was no mistaking it. One was General Ludendorff, the other Dr. Maru. Seizing the chance to end the German weapons program in one fell swoop, Steve lined up to strafe the car. But they must have had a driver waiting behind the wheel because it had already started to move. Before the general and the doctor could shut the doors, the vehicle was roaring out the gate. The side of the brick complex blocked Steve's shot and he had to abort. He didn't want to waste precious bullets.

Circling the installation, he watched the last of the slave labor force evacuate. The workers and their masters spread out in all directions, trying to get as far away from the factory as possible.

Sweeping down over the main building he blitzed the glass roof, sending it crashing down into the building. It was necessary for what he intended to do next. Cutting another tight turn, he lined up on the structure again. Holding the stick trapped between his knees, he armed a fifteen-pound hand bomb that was clipped to the inside of the cockpit. It had a contact fuse, which meant that to achieve full effect, it had to fall unimpeded through the roof and into the building before it struck something. He banked the Eindecker to gain altitude, this to avoid the resulting blast. He knew German hand bombs of this size would blow a crater fifteen feet wide and three feet deep. Eyeballing the drop, he hung the bomb outside the cockpit, and let go dead center of the structure. Immediately he banked hard left and pulled back on the *stick to gain even more altitude.*

A tremendous fireball erupted behind and below him. He felt both the heat and shock of the explosion, which blew the Fokker off course. Debris sailed past him, slicing into the plane's skin, and making it wobble. He turned west. With no pursuit to worry about, he trimmed back the throttle to get maximum distance out of his available fuel.

Steve Trevor's face strained as he again tried to fight the power of the lasso, and again failed.

"I was on my way back to London when the Germans shot me down," he said, his eyes locked onto the messenger bag resting at Hippolyta's feet.

Diana opened it, reached inside, and pulled out a green-bound notebook.

He nodded at it. "But if I can get those notes to British Intelligence in time …" His voice broke and he swallowed hard—the lasso was forcing him to reveal not just the facts but his feelings about them. "It can stop millions more from dying… Stop the war…"

"War? What war?" Diana said.

"The War To End All Wars. Four years, twenty-seven countries, twenty-five million dead—soldiers and civilians…" He swallowed again. The lasso was forcing him to reveal deep, painful truths. "Innocent people. Women and children, slaughtered. Their homes, villages: looted, burned. Weapons deadlier than you can imagine. Like nothing I've ever seen. It's like… the world is going to end." His voice was deep and he ground out the words, each one costing him dearly. Every piece of his soul cried out for him to stop this horrible massacre. He had to make them understand that he had a duty to the entire world. They had to set him free.

Standing behind the woman named Diana—the one who had saved his life—the Queen of these women wore such an expression of despair that he was certain he'd gotten though to her. *Yes, yes, you've got to let me go,* he silently told her.

Her face downcast, she said nothing.

He was at a loss.

It must be Ares who is doing this, Diana thought, flooding with dread. She could see the anguish in Steve Trevor's eyes. It mirrored theirs—the Amazons. He was a warrior, like them. He was trying to stop the God, as her mother had done. He was more like them than he, a human man, was not.

It was clear that Hippolyta wanted Diana to accompany her and her inner circle into the courtyard. Diana followed them out. Everyone was stunned, dismayed.

"Should we let him go?" Phillipus said.

Hippolyta's gaze was steely. "And risk him bringing more men to our shores? Phillipus…"

"Mother?" Diana tried to interrupt, but was ignored.

"We can't hold him forever, my Queen," Phillipus countered.

"Excuse me, Mother," Diana said, more firmly. "But after everything the man said, this must be Ares."

Everyone stopped and turned to stare at her.

"What are you talking about, child?" Senator Acantha said.

"Forgive me, Senator Acantha, but the man called it

'war without end.' Millions of people already dead. Like nothing he's ever seen. Only Ares could do such a thing. We cannot simply let him go. We must go with him."

There was a stir in the group. Surely she was not the only one to whom this had occurred.

"I will not deploy our army and leave Themyscira defenseless to go and fight their war," her mother said.

"This is not *their* war," Diana argued. She repeated the history lesson her mother had drilled into her night after night, gazing into the panel, brushing her hair.

"That was a story, Diana," Hippolyta bit off. "There is much you do not know. Men are easily corruptible." She spoke as if the matter was closed. But Diana was not put off.

"But Ares is behind that corruption," Diana reminded her. "It is Ares who has these Germans fighting. And stopping the God of War is our foreordinance. And now mankind must be freed. As Amazons, this is our duty." She looked to the others for agreement. But all eyes were focused on Hippolyta.

"But you are not an Amazon like the rest of us, Diana," her mother said.

The words cut her to the heart—not only because they were unjust, but because her mother was only using that as an excuse. Deflecting the point Diana was making. This was the entire reason Zeus had created the Amazons, was it not?

Was it not?

"So you will do nothing, as your Queen forbids it," Hippolyta ordered her. As if the matter was closed.

But it was not.

7

Diana sat on a low examination table in the Amazons' infirmary while Epione, a skilled healer, prepared to stitch up her arm. But after Epione had threaded the needle, the Amazon paused.

"Strange," she said. "You healed quickly."

Diana glanced down at her shoulder. Epione was right: the wound had closed up on its own. It was strange—or maybe it simply hadn't been that deep. There were far more pressing matters at hand.

"Is it true you saved his life?" Epione asked.

Diana shifted her attention. "Who told you that?"

"He did."

So her mother had sent him to be checked over. Diana took that as a good sign—and left the infirmary with the idea that she should check him over as well…

Plunging waterfalls cascaded from the roof of the cavern where Steve Trevor lounged in the topmost of four stacked bathing pools brimming with glowing blue water. He moved his foot through the water; the intensity of the color changed and he chuckled, intrigued. And as he rose naked from the water, in she walked.

Oh, good, she thought. *Now I can inspect him more closely.*

His injured shoulder had been bandaged, but the rest of his body was covered with lesser cuts and bruises, and old scars from other battles. So many scars. And as for the rest…

"Would you say you're a typical example of your sex?" she asked, approaching the pools.

He raised an eyebrow. "I am above average," he declared.

Diana's gaze dropped below his waist. "What is that?" she said, looking puzzled.

He flushed, then followed her eye line to the object that sat on the edge of the pool, on top of his clothes. "It's a watch," he said with apparent relief, scooping it up as he covered his front.

"A watch," Diana repeated.

"A watch. Tells time. My father gave it to me. Been through hell and back with him, and now it's with me, and good thing it's still ticking."

Diana took it from him and listened to its steady rhythm. "What for?"

"Because it tells time," he explained. "When to wake up, work, eat, sleep."

She chuckled. "You let this little thing tell you what to do?"

Steve took the watch from her and covered himself.

"Can I ask you some questions?"

She shrugged her consent, mildly curious about why he felt the need to display modesty but accepting his actions as his own.

He began. "Where are we?"

"Themyscira." There was no harm in telling him that. Besides, she already had.

His forehead wrinkled. "No, I got that before. I mean, where *are* we? Who are you people?" He gestured. "Why does the water do that? How come you don't know what a watch is? How can you speak English so well?"

"We speak hundreds of languages." Didn't he know anything about the Amazons? "We are the bridge of a greater understanding between all men."

He cocked his head as he gazed at her. "Right," he said neutrally, and paused. "Hey, I didn't get to say this earlier… but thank you for dragging me out of the water."

"Thank you for what you did on the beach."

A quick moment passed between them, one warrior to another acknowledging bravery on the field. That, and something more.

"So, are you going to let me go?" There was an edge to his voice, which she understood. Because the alternative…

She moved her shoulders. "I tried. It's not up to me. I even asked them to send me with you…"

His face brightened and Diana deflected.

"…or anyone. An Amazon. The Amazons."

"The Amazons?" he echoed. And then she was certain he had never heard of them. But how could that be?

"It is our sacred duty to defend the world, and I wish to go. But my mother will not allow it." She shaded her disappointment, her frustration.

"Can't say I blame her," he said. "The way this war is going, I wouldn't let anyone I care about near it."

"Then why do you want to go back?"

Steve started dressing. "I don't think 'want' is the word, but I've gotta try." He paused, then added, "My father used to say, 'You see something wrong in the world, you can either do nothing, or you can do something.' And I already tried nothing."

Diana was moved.

Moved, that is, to action.

I will honor Antiope, Diana thought. *I will fulfill my destiny.* The decision had been difficult, but it had been made.

Looming above all the other buildings of the village, back-lit by the light of the moon, the armory stood a silent sentinel over the Amazons' secret island. Diana surveyed the structure from the hill opposite, aware that guards were stationed on the other side. It was assumed that the building was unscalable—its outer surface of smooth stone interrupted by only shallow ledge, the structure banked by a depthless chasm far deeper than the one that she, as a little girl, had nearly leaped into. The window was her target—extremely high up.

A cow meandered nearby, contentedly chewing grass. Diana moved passed it and gave herself a long runway to build up speed for her leap. She braced herself, then took off running for a test. Five steps and she was running full speed, two more and the distance looked just about right. She planted her feet and made as if to jump. She wasn't sure it was possible.

Nevertheless, she jogged back to her starting point. Taking a couple of quick breaths, she paused for a second, then broke into an all-out sprint, legs driving, arms pumping. She hit the takeoff point perfectly and leapt over the abyss, hair flying behind her, soaring through the cool night.

The moonlit side of the building rushed towards her, closer and closer. The ledge loomed before her. Contact. She'd made it—

—but with one hand only. She was swinging back and forth, crazily. It was a very long way down. Then she held on with both hands, and she hung there for a moment, pleased with herself.

A crack. Beneath her weight, the ledge gave way.

She plummeted down the flat surface. There were no other ledges, nothing to hang onto. She tried nonetheless, seeking anything to grab, and drove her hand forward—

—straight into the stone. Her fist broke the brickwork; fragments tumbled as she took advantage of the handhold she had created, brows raised in surprise and relief. She swung back and forth for a second, then pushed her other hand into the dense stone. It punctured the thick rock as if it was made of honey cake. Another handhold.

She pulled out her hand, raised it up, and made another hole. Held on. Created another. Methodically smashing her hands knuckle-deep into the wall, she pulled herself up the entire height of the tower, finally making it to the window.

She hoisted herself up and balanced her weight on its thin edge. From there it was easy to drop down inside the armory. She landed lightly, barely making a sound. When her eyes adjusted to the dim light, the treasures of the armory snapped into focus. From its protective casing she took a shield. The heft was good, the workmanship exquisite. The Gods willing, it would deflect the projectiles of the rifles of men. The bullets.

Next she approached the Godkiller sword, which stood on its point in the exact center of the armory. Light filtered down on it, bathing it with an almost mystical glow. There she paused. The sword filled her vision. Her breath stopped. Her heart beat.

The Godkiller. The only weapon that could destroy Ares.

Take it, and she would dare to do that.

She would accept the destiny that now stood just beyond her reach. This was her last chance to turn back, her beckoning opportunity to seize the day. She understood the import of this moment, and the place it held in her story: the armory was holy ground, and this was the means to fulfill her sacred duty.

With her dying breath, Antiope herself had told her to take it. Mentor, teacher, savior. Diana gazed at the sword with awe and reverence. Let it be so, then.

Let it be so.

She reached into its ornate, sculpted cradle and grasped it. The rightness of the grip; she felt something now, an amplification of the whispery sensation she had felt when her mother had first shown it to her. *Who will wield it?*

I.

She held it up. Moonlight streaming through the high window hit the blade and the reflected flashes spiraled dizzyingly around the room. Perhaps as a result of its perfect balance, the Godkiller seemed to float weightless in her hand, as if it had been created just for her.

That is what I am doing, she thought. Her skin prickled with anxiety even as a thrill of excitement fanned outward from the base of her spine. *I am going on a quest to save the world.*

To her left, armor gleamed red, blue, white, gold. The armor of a warrior. And the Lasso of Hestia, which had revealed her quest to her through the mouthpiece of the man. Steve Trevor.

Diana left the armory. Keeping to the shadows, away from the guards, she descended the hillside with her bounty. She changed and made all ready, saddling horses, and preparing herself to step into history.

As was her foreordinance.

Dressed in a heavy wool cloak, Diana entered Steve's chamber to find him studying a map. He held a compass. He looked at her and said, "Nice outfit."

"Thank you," she said briskly. Speed was imperative. "Now I will show you the way off the island. And you will take me to Ares."

He gave her a measured look as if he couldn't quite believe his ears. He must have sensed her determination—and her competence—as he nodded and said, "Deal."

He rose and placed his belongings—the green book as well—into his messenger bag. His moved sparely; he was focused but calm. For all she knew, she was leading him away from death—or toward her own.

Diana led him out of the infirmary to the trees where

the two Amazon warhorses she had saddled chuffed at her approach. He climbed onto his mount with a confidence and style that made her smile. Steve was obviously a horseman as well as a pilot and a spy. A versatile companion for as far as their journey took the two of them together.

They rode silently through dark, dense forest. Diana followed a well-worn trail between the tall trees, urging her horse to go faster. There wasn't much light to see by, but the animals were biddable. Steve kept up the pace, staying right behind her.

They emerged from the forest at the edge of a small, protected harbor. Moonlight danced on the wind-riffled water. She waved him onward and they followed the curve of the shore. She stopped at the bow of an Amazon sailing vessel. It was very unlike the German warship, more like the small boats the Germans had used to land on the beach, although it had sails and its wooden hull was embellished with intricate carvings.

"We're leaving in that?" Steve said.

"We are."

"We're leaving in that," he repeated.

"Do you not know how to sail?" Diana asked him as they both dismounted.

"Of course I know how to sail," Steve said. "Why wouldn't I be able to sail? It's just been a while." He hesitated. And then his eyes widened.

"What?" Diana said.

As he pointed at the valley behind them, she heard the thunder of horses' hooves and turned. Hippolyta and the Queen's guard were moving in their direction, the guards holding torches. From this distance, Diana couldn't make out her mother's expression, but the Queen sat tall in her saddle. Diana had always respected her mother, but just then, the tiniest bit of fear insinuated itself as she prepared to defend her actions. For his part, Steve watched carefully. Diana wondered if he was formulating an escape plan. Did he have a gun? Would he shoot any of the Amazons in order to get free? It was not a scenario she had considered, and she wished she had searched him.

Hippolyta raised her hand as they drew near and the guards reined in their mounts. She jumped down from her horse and approached Diana alone.

Diana took a quick breath. She looked into her mother's eyes and said, "I am going, Mother. I can't stand by while innocent lives are lost. If no one else will defend the world from Ares, I must. I must go—"

"I know," Hippolyta said.

There was no fury in her mother's face, only sadness. Deep sadness.

"Or at least I know I cannot stop you," the Queen corrected herself. "There is so much—so much you do not understand."

"I understand enough," Diana said. "That I am willing to fight for those who cannot fight for themselves. Like you once did." She hoped for a response from her mother, an admission that she was right. But the Queen remained sorrowful as she gazed at her child.

"You know that if you choose to leave us, you may never return." Her voice broke.

Diana's throat tightened. *Never* for an Amazon was an eternity.

"Who will I be if I stay?" she asked, searching her mother's face.

Hippolyta gazed at her with deep love. Then the Queen reached over to her horse and pulled something shiny from the saddlebag. Diana's breath caught. It was Antiope's headband, with its inverted triangle and sunburst.

Her voice husky with emotion, Hippolyta said, "This belonged to the greatest warrior in our history—make sure you are worthy of it."

"I will," Diana said, equally moved. This was their leave taking, their farewell. Everything she had ever known... her beloved mother, the Amazons: Antiope, Orana. The constellations overhead: tears, guideposts. A gentle wind, the moonlight, soft. The parting... so hard. So very hard. But right.

Hippolyta took a deep breath and gazed with eyes that saw Diana, really saw her for what she had become. Besides tenderness, there was respect. Pride. Diana had her Queen's blessing. Her mother's love.

"Be careful in the world of men, Diana. They do not deserve you," Hippolyta said.

All those nights braiding hair, giggling, listening to the stories of the Amazons, seeing the real love the people bore for her mother, and for her... In the throes of parting, she sought to lock the treasures of her girlhood away in her heart.

"You have been my greatest love." Her mother's eyes overflowed with tears and she cradled Diana's face in her hands. "Today you are my greatest sorrow."

This face, forever. Her mother's hands, forever.

One last look, and then Diana turned and walked away. Away from the only home, the only family she had ever known. Towards Steve and the ship, and her future. Her heart was heavy as she cast off the mooring lines and, with Steve's help, raised the sails. The boat began to move at once, pushed by a following wind. She looked back from the stern. She could see the torches still on the beach, points of light that got smaller and smaller. Mists enfolded Themyscira, her homeland, and the barrier that protected the island from the eyes of the men.

And from her own eyes now.

Menalippe approached her queen, who stood unmoving like a statue, facing the sea. The tiny dot that was Diana's ship was still visible, and Hippolyta would stare after it for a hundred years if it still bobbed on the waves. It would be impossible to convey the enormity of her sorrow, the vastness of her fear, and the depth of her pride in her daughter.

"Should you have told her?" Menalippe asked.

Hippolyta had considered that question. Wrestled with it. And ultimately rejected it.

"The more she knows," Hippolyta said, "the faster he will find her."

BOOK II

WARRIOR

"It is only the dead who have seen the end of war."

—Attributed to Plato

8

Themyscira was gone. Let it be so, then. After taking a few moments, Diana put thoughts of home aside and focused on her quest. As she and Steve Trevor balanced with the rocking of the waves beneath the bow, she said, "How long until we reach the war?"

He considered. "The war? Which part? The Eastern Front in France is four hundred miles long—from the Alps to the Atlantic."

She thought a moment. "Where the fighting is the most intense, then. If you take me there, I am sure I'll find Ares."

There was a beat. Then he said, "Ares? As in the God of War?"

She nodded. "The God of War is our responsibility. Only an Amazon can defeat him. With this. "

She drew the Godkiller from beneath her cloak and ran her hand reverently along the blade. The ancient runes gleamed in the starlight. "And once I do, the war will end."

He looked from the massive sword to her. "Look, I

appreciate your spirit, but this war's a great big mess and there's not a whole lot we can do about it. But we can try to get to the men who can."

"I am the man who can," she countered. "And after I find and destroy Ares, the German armies will be freed from his influence—and there will be good men again, and the world will be better."

Another hesitation, and then he said, "Great."

She detected no sarcasm in his tone and decided to take him at face value—at least for the time being. She needed him. The sails lofted; the waves rolled in the vastness of this unknown sea. She watched as he began to move bundles around, then gathered up and spread out a blanket.

"What are you doing?" she asked him.

"I thought maybe you'd want to get some sleep."

That was sensible. And thoughtful. But sleeping in close quarters in his presence? She hadn't considered that. "What about you? Are you not sleeping? Does the average man not sleep?"

He continued to arrange the bed clothing with a preoccupied air, then turned to her. "Yes, we sleep. We just don't sleep with…" He trailed off, not looking at her.

When he didn't finish his thought, she said, "You don't sleep with women?" It was a reasonable conclusion. But speaking of it made her feel odd. Feeling a bit conspicuous, she lay down on the bed he had made for her and took a few moments to adjust her cloak around herself.

"I mean, I do sleep with—I sleep with women, yes." He, too, seemed a bit flustered. "Yes I do," he said emphatically, raising his eyes to the stars. "But out of the confines of marriage, it's not polite to assume—"

"Marriage?" she interjected, unfamiliar with the word. She had not come across it in her studies.

"You don't have that down in… yeah," he said. He thought a moment. "You go before a judge, and you swear to love, cherish, and honor each other until death you do part."

He reclined on a sack he had placed over the lines of the boat some distance from her. He was pointedly not looking at her; she slid a sideways glance at him, then looked away. "Do they? Do they love each other until death?"

"Not very often," he conceded.

"Then why do they do it?"

Cocking his head, he seemed to fix his attention on the one star in particular. "I… have no idea."

She cocked a brow, less certain of navigating this conversation than she was of scaling the smooth surface of the armory tower. "So you cannot sleep with me unless we are married?" She had a lot to learn about the world of mankind, that was clear.

"I'll sleep with you," he said quickly, glancing at her, then back up at the sky. "I'll sleep with you if you want."

She gestured to the empty space beside her. "There's plenty of room. It's up to—"

"—If you don't mind," he said, speaking over her.

"— you," she finished, as he continued.

"—I'll come sleep with you. I'll make the choice. I'll come sleep with you."

The fumbling way they spoke over each other dissolved into an awkward silence as he stretched out beside her. She felt his warmth, and her situation hit home—she was on a Themyscira fishing boat in the middle of an ocean with a man. It was not the evening she had envisioned upon waking. But then, nothing had gone as expected this day.

The boat rocked. She kept her focus up at the stars, finding it simpler than making eye contact with him, and toyed with the end of her cloak, not quite certain what to say next. Apparently, neither was he.

Then, after a time, he shifted his position very slightly. "Okay. Where I come from, I am not considered average," he said. Another pause. "You know, uh, being a spy, you need to show a certain amount of vigor." He raised his fists up slightly in a gesture of strength. She was content to listen. "You never met a man before." It sounded as if he were having trouble understanding that. "What about your father?"

"I had no father. My mother sculpted me from clay. I was brought to life by Zeus."

"Well, that's… neat."

He still sounded a bit uncertain about her. Well, she was not certain of him, either. She stretched to get more comfortable, touching him accidentally. He jumped.

"Sorry," she said, and he nodded. They both continued to study the stars. The constellations had not altered in the minutes the two had kept watch over them.

"Where I come from, babies are made differently," he ventured.

"You refer to reproductive biology," she said simply.

"Yes."

"I know. I know all about that," she said.

"I refer to that and… other things." They were starting to overlap their sentences again—like lapping waves of words rising and falling into each other.

"Ah," Diana said. "The pleasures of the flesh."

Steve shifted. "You know about that?"

"Of course," Diana replied. "I've read all twelve volumes of Clio's *Treatises on Bodily Pleasure*."

He smiled faintly. "All twelve, huh? You bring any of them with you?"

She raised a brow. "You would not enjoy them."

"I don't know. Maybe. Why not?"

"They came to the conclusion that men are essential for procreation, but when it comes to pleasure… unnecessary."

"No. No." His voice trailed off.

More silence. Aware that they were floundering again, Diana said, "Good night," and turned away from him to find some peace

"Good night," he replied politely.

The boat sailed on into the dark.

German airfield
Belgium

General Ludendorff marched across the airfield, which was dotted with aircraft, toward the hanger that was the site of Dr. Maru's new factory. He was followed by a captain and a handful of uniformed guards. His hopes for this visit were high, his expectations enormous. Dr. Maru was his most capable scientist, the Fatherland's secret weapon. She must not disappoint him today. A man in the desert could not be more thirsty for the life-saving water of victory. The world in turmoil had hardened and strengthened many courageous souls, raising and ennobling them to heights they had not dreamed of—and those men must acknowledge that he, Ludendorff, deserved the credit. He had pushed for this war, this noble cause that made demands of men unmatched by any other endeavor; this quest that had opened doors to scientific advances so astonishing they bordered on myth. War was glorious. *Rise up, warriors. Take your stand!* So wrote Sparta's great poet, Tyrtaeus, back in the dawn of mankind, armies chorusing his songs praising valor and courage in battle.

Only through the extreme pressure of danger could men progress; the white-hot flames of peril tempered their spines to steel. The bigger the contest, the greater the growth—the weak weeded out, the cowardly dispatched. Rising from the chaff: better men.

He would thresh the fields of battle. And Dr. Maru, with all her lethal poisons and liberating discoveries, would ensure that only the finest survived—the elite of mankind, freed from the sucking pit filled with the lesser men than they.

This was his quest; he needed weapons to match his ambitions. Dr. Maru must make them for him. She *must*.

The converted hangar was a cold, draughty building filled with machinery and workers who picked up their pace the moment they saw him striding in. That was both disturbing and pleasing—he would have preferred that they were already working at their full capacity before his presence triggered an increase in effort. However, it was good to be feared.

"How long until we are operational?" he asked the captain.

With an air of cautious pride, the captain replied, "Two days, sir."

"You have until tonight, Captain."

The man blanched. "Sir, the men have had no food. No sleep."

Ludendorff glared at him. "Do you think I've had food or rest, Captain? Do you hear me making excuses? Your men are weak. Complacent. You've let them forget that an attack can come at any time, from any quarter. So let's you and I remind them, shall we?"

Ludendorff drew his Luger and, without another word, shot the captain in the head. All eyes turned as the lifeless man's body hit the ground with a thud. Shock coursed through the onlookers like an electric jolt.

Satisfied that he had made his point, Ludendorff strode into the hangar. It was large, dirty, busy. Caustic chemicals singed his nostrils. His blood sang.

He headed for Dr. Maru's new laboratory. Barrels of chemical agents and equipment lined the walls. Dr. Maru was bent over a table, writing furiously in a new notebook. Wadded-up papers were strewn over her workstation. She seemed panicky, frustrated. Not a good sign.

"General," she said, looking up, almost fearfully.

"Doctor, progress?" he said.

The look on her face told him she was struggling. He masked his frustration and waited for her answer.

"Not enough," she reluctantly confessed, and then gave up all semblance of adequacy. "It's over, General. Germany is giving up. Von Hindenburg has recommended the Kaiser sign the Armistice. We have run out of time."

Von Hindenburg. That gutless waste of space. Outwardly calm, inwardly fuming, he shrugged in disagreement. "As soon as the Kaiser sees the newest weapon, he will not sign the Armistice."

Maru's dark eyes flashed with concern. "But without my book—"

"We will get your book." He caressed her face, from fingertips to her skin to the flesh-colored plates covering the damage. So brilliant, and yet, quite fragile in her way. A woman with her feelings that must be attended to if he was to get what he wanted. It was a trifling matter to cajole and encourage her, and the results were well worth it. When it came to creating revolutionary weapons, she was a true genius. He had not seen her equal in all his long life.

"It's you I believe in," he said softly. "Not it. I know that you can and will succeed."

She blushed under his gaze, and he pressed his advantage. "Great victories require great sacrifices," he said. "And you've sacrificed so much." Her face had been badly scarred in a laboratory explosion, and men who had seen worse injuries in battle turned away at the sight of her bare face. He leaned closer and whispered in her ear, "I believe in you."

She pulled back from him. The look in her eyes changed—brighter, more confident. He had inspired her to great heights before, and her mercurial change in attitude reassured him. Her battlefield was science, and she was a true warrior for the cause.

"It was what you were put on this earth to do," he added, one final push to keep her focused on success.

She nodded, said eagerly, "Something did come to me last night. A different kind of gas." She turned away, then plucked up and handed him a blue capsule. "To restore your strength."

These capsules were a stunning achievement. In eager

anticipation, Ludendorff held the capsule under his nose and cracked it open between his thumbs. He inhaled the sharp vapor. A shiver of stinging pain shot through his body like an explosion. He staggered, reaching out for the edge of the table for support. The veins in his face and neck pulsated, his heart to roar. His lips drew back from his teeth in a feral snarl and he was flooded to bursting with energy, raw power. Stamina, vitality—forces he knew well, and loved. Shaking, he took out his pistol. In front of the doctor, he crushed it with his bare hand as if it were made of paper. The barrel made a most satisfying crunch as he flattened it.

If she could do this, she could do anything.

He smiled and nodded to Dr. Maru, who had stood by, observing. She was enthralled by the success of the vapor. Then a light came on and she gazed at her crumpled up papers; grabbing one of them, she unfolded it, studied it, and blinked.

"I've got it. I've got it," she said. Her face glowed with exultation. "And if it's what I think, it's going to be terrible."

Dreams of a race through the marketplace. Mnemosyne calling, "Diana, come back here!"

Aboard the Amazonian vessel, Diana awoke. The sky above the river Thames floated gray and viscous, choked with haze from a hundred-hundred smokestacks. London was one gigantic industrial complex of munitions factories, salvage shops, and repair facilities.

She sat up. The river was crowded with strange, noisy vessels belching black smoke into the dreary, overcast sky. The water smelled like rotting garbage.

On either side of the boat, the riverbanks were

clogged with enormous buildings of stone, towers and chimneys spewing coal smoke—a stench so thick it coated her throat and made her eyes water. Bridges spanned the foul currents, the filth spilling into the sea. Horses, conveyances, and people crossed the bridges and crammed the docksides. They were *everywhere*.

"Good morning," Steve said. "We got lucky, caught a ride. Made good time."

Caught a ride? Towed them, then?

"Welcome to jolly ol' London," he said.

She took in the city's skyline, the bridges, the quays, remembering the beauty of Themyscira with a pang—and fresh determination. War had done this to this city. Once Ares was dead, it would become habitable again.

"It's hideous," she said bluntly.

Mildly amused, appreciative of her frankness, Steve took in Whitehall—the Houses of Parliament—and St. Paul's Cathedral. It would be difficult for her to comprehend the sense of relief this skyline engendered in him. She had lived in an untouched Eden. But for him, this had pretty much become home—if a spy in the middle of a war actually had a home. A home base, then. Same for her, since she couldn't return to Themyscira. She must be going through six hundred kinds of culture shock. She had stepped into this world of her own volition, but it had to be hard for her to deal with. He felt for her.

"Eh, it's not for everyone," he deadpanned.

They disembarked, leaving Diana's vessel in the care of a bemused riverman. As they walked the London streets to Piccadilly Circus, Diana stared with disbelieving eyes at the bedlam. Trash snapping at the curbs, thin little boys hawking newspapers, two women knocking broad hats festooned with feathers and ribbons as they chatted, attempting to hear each over the din. Mingling with the haze, an overlay of rushing colorlessness—everyone hurrying—some of that caused by the stress of war, Diana was sure, but as for the rest, this was the sizzling world of modern humanity. This was not the easy country landscape of her mother's history of the Amazons, but something that weighted down the land and water through the hands of mankind. The intrusion of centuries of civilization that the Amazons had not witnessed. She was the only one of her people to see it.

An amazing number of heavily dressed people clogged the walking paths. Horse-drawn carts vied with motorized vehicles; shop placards clamored for attention and signs on buildings exhorted people to buy war bonds. On every corner, newspaper headlines shouted about war and votes for women.

This was the world Ares had handed these people.

And yet there were wonders to behold. The scent of fresh bread, the aerial dance of a hundred pigeons, a street performer making a show of escaping a complicated rig of chains and locks as pedestrians halted their progress to watch. Despite the direness of their situation, people smiled at one another.

A carriage without a horse honked at her and Diana was about to move out of its way when Steve protectively pulled her aside. She turned to watch it drive off, a faint grin on her face. A group of men in uniforms grouped around a truck stirred as she passed; a few of them hooted, called out to her.

"Gentlemen, eyes to yourself," Steve chided them. "Thank you so much." Diana had moved ahead and he called out, "Diana!"

She slowed; they came abreast. Ahead of them a man and a woman walked hand in hand.

"Why are they holding hands?" she asked Steve.

He gestured to the couple with his head. "Well, because they're… together."

Diana reached out and took his hand. He gently eased himself free, not wishing to cause offense.

"No," he said, "we're not together… I mean, in this way." He gestured. "Look, we need to go this way."

She faced him. Enough exploration. She had a mission and it was time to get down to business. "Because this is the way to the war?"

"Technically, that's the way to the war," he said, pointing in the opposite direction.

Her brows shot up. "Then where are we going?"

He patted his messenger bag. "I have to get this notebook to my superiors."

She narrowed her eyes. "No, no, no, no, no. I let you go, you take me to Ares. We made a deal, Steve Trevor. A deal is a promise. A promise is unbreakable." She looked him in the eyes, hard, and held onto the collar of his jacket.

"Yeah, oh, boy," he said, with a quick grimace. She was as driven as he was; intractable, one might say. "Okay… come with me to deliver this first, then we'll get you a ticket to the war."

Faced with no other choice, she walked on with him.

* * *

It was easy to blend into the street traffic.

The man with the mustache kept his long coat wrapped around his body and shadowed Steve Trevor, the American who was working for the British.

The American who had stolen the Fatherland's secrets.

The man was charged with retrieving what Trevor had taken by any means necessary—including murder. Assassination, more politely put, in the shadow game of spies and their masters. He didn't know who the dark-haired, strangely attired woman was, but no matter; she was expendable.

As he walked, a nursemaid pushing a perambulator jostled him. He wasn't alone on the streets of London.

Oh, no. He was far from alone.

Steve glanced at the looks thrown Diana's way. Her woolen cloak fell open on occasion, revealing her skimpy Amazonian armor and greaves. Aiming for tact, he said, "I need to change. And you…" He pulled the edges of her cloak together, manfully resisting the opportunity to peek at her long, lithe body.

"What are you doing?" she asked him.

"Let's go buy you some clothes."

"Why?"

"Because you aren't wearing any."

She looked down at her armor, then at the women on the street.

"What do these women wear into battle?" she asked.

Where to even begin? "Well, women don't exactly…"

Diana turned her attention to a young mother

holding an infant. "A baby!" she exclaimed, swooping toward them. Steve grabbed her arm.

"No babies, no babies," Steve half-pleaded. "And that one is not made of clay," Steve said, taking her gently by the arm and leading her down the crowded sidewalk. "Diana, please."

About thirty paces behind them, a short, round man in a derby hat, suit and woolen overcoat followed unobtrusively. There was nothing notable about him, nothing that drew attention. He looked perfectly British. He could have been a clerk from a haberdashery or a bookkeeper or a thread salesman. Bland as bland could be, right down to his neatly trimmed, pale ginger beard. One had to look closely to see the hard glint in his small, wide-set eyes. Hurrying to keep up with his quarry, he felt the comforting weight of the loaded revolver in his coat pocket.

Selfridges, the magnificent department store where all manner of expensive goods could be bought, had been open for nearly a decade when Steve and Diana went in through its Art Nouveau entrance. The difference between it and the marketplace of Themyscira could not have been more pronounced and though he was in a hurry, Steve appreciated Diana's impulse to gawk. Everything from Tiffany lamps to opera glasses could be purchased at Selfridges.

As planned, Etta Candy was waiting for them in the women's fashions department. A gray hat decorated with organdy rosettes sat atop her ginger hair and she was wearing an empire-waisted checked jacket over a long straight skirt and boots. In Steve's opinion, it was a perfect ensemble for Diana to pass as a regular woman.

Etta brightened when she saw the two of them. "Thank God!" she cried. "You're not dead."

Diana looked at Steve.

"I did think you were dead this time, I really did, then I got your call…" She turned to Diana and said, "He was gone for weeks! Not a single word. Very unlike him." She extended her hand toward Diana. "Let me introduce myself. I'm Etta Candy, Captain Trevor's secretary."

Diana stopped short and looked at her.

"What's a secretary?" Diana asked.

Etta shrugged. "Well, I do everything. I go where he tells me to go and I do what he tells me to do."

Diana cocked a brow. "Where I'm from," she said, "that's called slavery."

Etta blinked. "Ooh, I really like her," she breathed. "I do. I like her."

"Ladies," Steve said.

The secretary eyed Diana's clothing. "We've got our work cut out for us," she said brightly as they moved forward.

Diana was struck by a dizzying chorus of sweet scents. All around her were reflective surfaces, glass cases, chandeliers, polished marble floors and pillars. With towering ceilings, it looked like a palace, but unlike her family's royal residence, it was full of things. Clothing. Jewelry. Linens. Accessories. Food stuffs. The sheer number of objects on display and their artful presentation were overwhelming.

Diana decided to focus on one thing at a time. She stopped in front of a mannequin of a woman dressed in a tight-fitting, fabric corset from bosom to mid-thigh.

"Is this what passes for armor in your country?" she asked Etta.

"Of a sort," Etta said. "It's fashion. Keeps our tummies in."

"Why must you keep them in?"

Etta sighed. "Only a woman with no tummy would ask that question." She held up an outfit for Diana to consider. Gray and rather baggy. "Conservative, but not entirely… unfun."

Diana gave Steve a *Do I have to?* look.

"Try it on, at least," Steve said.

"Very well." It was her turn to sigh.

Then she started to take off her cloak. Etta's eyes went wide and she rushed over to stop her from removing it.

As she led her away, Etta shot Steve a questioning look, as if to say, *Where did you find this woman?*

After putting on the outfit Diana stepped up to a full-length mirror. The garment was frilly, its layers upon layers of fabric giving her the look of a puffy cloud, the matching cap completing the illusion. It was ridiculous.

"How can a woman possibly fight in this?" she said, executing a side kick. She took off the hat and sniffed it.

"Fight? We use our principles," Etta told her. "It's how we're going to get the vote. Not that I'm opposed to engaging in a bit of fisticuffs should the occasion arise." With a twinkle in her eye, she limply positioned her hands for combat.

Diana went back behind the curtain to try on the second of Etta's suggestions. Both the white blouse with its scarf such as the men wore and the dark skirt were quite tight.

Etta admired the fit and said, "Lovely."

Diana tested the outfit by trying a front snap kick. It was impossible to kick higher than a shin in the dress, and the attempt caused the back seam to rip open. She shook her head at Etta: It just wouldn't do.

The third choice was a virtual copy of what Etta herself was wearing. Diana yanked at the lace collar impatiently. "So itchy," she complained. "And it's choking me."

"I can't say that I blame it," Etta muttered.

Diana returned to the changing room and began to put on yet another ensemble. She was nearly finished when through the velvet curtain she heard Steve's voice as he walked up to Etta. "Where is she?" he said.

"Trying on outfit number two-hundred and twenty-six."

Diana stepped from the changing room with her hair pulled back in a fashionable coil, dressed in a belted gray suit, black boots and a black felt hat. On any other woman the outfit would have been stylish, pleasant, but unremarkable. But on her, well...

Well. Steve himself had bought new clothes. He wore a wide-brimmed, dark gray fedora that matched his new tweed suit, a white shirt with a stiff collar and tie accented with a vest. Over that, a trench coat. It wasn't difficult to remember the shape of his body beneath all the fabric, but she was bemused once again by how much clothing these people found necessary.

Diana shifted uncomfortably, disliking the restrictions

the garment placed on her. Steve seemed to be staring at it fixedly, then snapped out of it.

He turned to Etta. "Miss Candy, the whole point was to make her *less* distracting," he said.

Steve looked around the store, apparently searching for something. He moved to a nearby counter and picked up a pair of glasses. He gently put the glasses on Diana's face. The lenses were plain glass so she could see perfectly through them. He stepped back to examine her and seemed very satisfied.

"Really, specs?" Etta said wryly. "And suddenly she's not the most beautiful woman you've ever seen?"

Diana looked into the mirror, took a deep breath, and settled into the clothes. The corners of her mouth turned up in a little smile as she adjusted her glasses. An effective way to blend in, she supposed. One must do what one must do.

With her hair up, in her glasses and new outfit, she picked up her sword and shield. The trio descended a short flight of stairs toward a revolving door. Diana crashed into it then backed up. Her sword caught.

Steve reached to help her, but Diana demurred.

"Let me try it by myself," she said. She gauged the speed of the door's turns, then stepped inside and exited successfully. In concert, Steve and Etta attempted to take her sword away.

Etta said cheerfully, "Why don't I meet you at the office. Meanwhile—" she reached for the sword "—I'll take this for safekeeping."

Diana refused, brandishing the sword. But she was aware that people were staring at her. No one else on the street was armed with sword and shield. The point was for them to blend in so that Steve could deliver the notebook and take her to the Front.

"Diana, put the sword down, please," Steve said.

"It doesn't go with the outfit," Etta said.

"At all," Steve added.

It galled her to give up her weapons in this strange place. At least she had the Lasso of Hestia in the pocket of her jacket. "Promise that you will protect it with your life?" She was stern.

Etta nodded, but Diana wasn't certain that she could trust her.

"Hand that over," Steve insisted.

Diana let them take the sword.

"Shield." Etta was insistent.

Diana relented. Etta struggled under the awkwardness of her parcels—Amazonian sword, shield, and shopping bag. The cloak alone weighed as much as a boat anchor, or nearly so.

"Thanks, Etta. See you soon," Steve said.

What on earth, Etta thought. She watched this Diana, champion to secretaries everywhere, walk on down the street with Captain Trevor. Charming yet... eccentric.

Then her gaze ticked to a bearded man who seemed to be following the pair. Etta frowned.

And kept watching.

After they took their leave, Diana and Steve continued down Oxford Street. A few blocks on, Steve glanced over his shoulder and stiffened.

"What is it?" she asked.

"Hopefully nothing," he replied, then steered her into an ally.

She looked up at him. "Steve, why are we hiding?"

"Ssh," he cautioned. "Come on."

He turned; a man stepped from the shadows, pointing a gun at Steve's head.

"Captain Trevor," he said in a thick German accent, "I believe you have something that is the property of General Ludendorff."

Diana now knew what guns could do. Aware of the danger she and Steve were in, she waited for an opening to attack. The man waved the gun threateningly and backed the two of them deeper into the alley. There were two more men there. Another two joined.

That made five adversaries—three of whom had their guns out.

"Ah. It's the bad guy convention," Steve said.

"Give us Dr. Maru's notebook," the man snapped.

Steve moved in front of Diana as if trying to block her from the line of fire. He patted his coat pockets. "Where did I put that thing?"

Stepping in front of her got him that much closer to the man with his finger on the trigger. Steve head-butted their primary attacker, who fell back. When Diana started to advance, Steve held up his arm protectively.

"Stay behind me!" he shouted.

The gunman fired. Diana swung her right arm up in front of him. It was not a conscious act. It was automatic, reactive, as if her body knew something she didn't. With a loud crack and a spark the shot ricocheted off her bracelet. Steve opened his hand, revealing a piece of the bullet in his palm.

The German spies and Steve looked at her in astonishment.

"Or maybe not," Steve said.

The gunman examined his pistol, then pulled the trigger again. One of the men blocking the alleyway fired at them almost simultaneously. Diana's reflexes sped up, which made it seem like the bullets were slowing down. She raised both bracelets, easily deflecting the bullets to either side. One went high, the other low. They surrounded her, shooting in all directions. She spun, deflecting every projectile. Her glasses whipped off, were crushed underfoot.

Steve knocked aside the weapon of a mustachioed attacker and slammed his forearm into the man's throat. The man dropped his weapon, choking, clutching his neck with both hands. He backed up until he hit the alley wall, then Steve punched him with a straight right that snapped back his head and slammed it into the bricks.

The bearded man had wheeled around and was trying to get a shot at Steve. Diana grabbed the barrel and twisted it up. The shot went off harmlessly in the air. The German reached for something in his left coat sleeve, but before he could grab it, Diana smashed her bracelet into the side of his head. His hat went flying and as he fell to the wet pavement, his eyes rolled back in his head.

The remaining gunman got off one shot at close range. But close or far didn't matter to Diana. The bullet crawled towards her and she knocked it aside with her bracelet.

"Is there anything else you want to show me?" Steve said in amazement.

She smiled at him victoriously. She had a feeling that there were more surprises to come.

The last three spies summoned their courage and rushed Diana and Steve all at once, hoping to overwhelm them. Neither of their targets budged. Diana slammed her fist into the face of the man leading the charge. The combination of his momentum and her compact punch sent him sprawling to the cobblestones. Steve took on the next attacker, blocking a big roundhouse swing and stepping into his counterblow. The impact of fist against chin lifted the man off his feet and he crashed flat on his back.

The second to the last gunman standing clicked his weapon; he had run out of bullets. *Click click click,* he stared at the useless gun.

"Tough luck," Steve said. He punched him and the man dropped.

Their last attacker—the man with the beard—made a run for it, but Etta appeared, blocking him.

"I thought you looked suspicious," she said.

Diana whipped out the Lasso of Hestia and caught him by the leg. He fell to the ground. The lasso began to glow as Diana knelt at his side. His eyes were wild. She put a compassionate hand on his chest. In her mind, his actions were not his own. He was a puppet of the God of War.

"I am sorry," she said. "You are clearly under his control. Let me help you get free. Where will I find Ares?"

But before the power of the Lasso could take full control, the spy popped something between his teeth and bit down. She caught a whiff of bitter almonds as his body fell into a violent seizure. It was over in seconds.

"He's dead," she said, looking up at Steve and Etta.

"Cyanide," Steve filled in.

The dead man's mouth foamed. Diana silently promised him that Ares would pay for his death. She gazed up at the dirty London sky.

For that, and so much else.

9

Because of the attack, Steve's movements through the city took on more urgency; Diana kept pace easily with him. Throughout the city, horns blared; the populace was anxious, busy. They reached the War Office, an enormous building filled with people who were employed in every aspect of war, from tactical decisions to provisioning Britain's three enormous armies—combined, a total of four million men.

They entered the vast edifice with its marble floors and stairways, and domes flowing with watery English sunlight, reminding her very little of the council chambers back home. The only war council held in recent memory had been the one in which Diana argued for Steve's life to be spared.

Steve pulled back one of the heavy double doors leading to the assembly hall. It was not a huge room, clubby and stuffy with rows of seats on either side of the main aisle behind heavy wooden bannisters. There were paintings of men in stupendous hats on the walls. The occupants were all male, some dressed in military uniforms resembling Steve's German uniform, decorated with rows of ribbons, only made from fabric in shades of brown; others wore tailored three-piece suits such as he wore now. The object of their ire was a kindly looking man, older than Steve, but not as old as some others in the hall.

"Stay here," Steve said.

Diana nodded that she would. But as soon as he started down the central aisle, she proceeded to follow him, running her hand over the bannister, smiling at the dumbfounded men who were staring at her.

"Gentlemen," said the small man. "Germany is an immensely proud nation who will never surrender. The only way to end this war and restore world peace is to negotiate an armistice."

The majority of the assembly roared its disapproval. Diana took note—peace was an unpopular subject. More evidence of Ares's meddling.

Steve seemed to be looking for someone in the audience. He leaned over the rail and said, "Colonel!"

Six men in nearly identical uniforms turned their heads to look at him.

"Sorry," Steve said. "Colonel!"

Another uniformed man turned his way. He had white hair and rows of medals on his chest and he appeared amazed and relieved to see Steve. Steve nodded towards the exit, indicating the need for a private word.

The small man pressed on, addressing the group. "Our only aim at this moment must be to achieve peace at any cost."

That brought another roar of disapproval. Then, as Steve and Diana entered more deeply into the room, the cries momentarily died down. She understood at once that they were taken aback that a woman had entered their sacred domain. Diana chose not to take umbrage. This was not her world and Steve needed to find the correct person to give the notebook to. Then he could get her to the Front.

Finally Steve took her arm and led her out of the assembly room, murmuring, "Sorry, excuse me…"

The discussion resumed. Through the open door Diana could hear the man insisting, "Gentlemen, I beg you, please, if you'll just hear me out…"

"Why will they not let him speak?" Diana said, pulling open the door to the assembly room to observe. "He's talking peace."

The white-haired man followed them into the hallway. "Trevor?" he began. "What the hell were you thinking bringing a woman into the council chamber?"

Though indignant, Diana kept her cool and said nothing, preferring to attend to the immediate matter. Steve held up his hand for calm, then addressed the colonel. "I'm sorry, Colonel Darnell, but the intel I've brought back is very time sensitive. We need to get it to cryptography. And I need an immediate audience with the generals…"

Speaking over Steve, the man said, "You don't just barge in here like this and demand an audience with the cabinet. Cryptography takes time and…"

Steve was persistent. "Sir, with all due respect, if what I saw—"

The small, older man who had been arguing for peace walked out of the chamber through the doorway. "Captain Trevor!" he said. "I'd heard you were lost on one of your missions, yet here you are. And you've brought a friend."

He smiled pleasantly at Diana, and she smiled back. She preferred him to the challenging warrior who seemed more interested in placing obstacles in Steve's way rather than listening to what his own spy had to tell him.

Steve inclined his head. "Our deepest apologies for the interruption, Sir—"

"Nonsense," the man cut in. "Thanks to this young woman, the room was finally quiet enough for me to get a few words in." He made a humble bow to Diana and added, "Sir Patrick Morgan, at your service."

Diana inclined her head in response. "Diana," she said. "Princess of…"

Steve broke in before she could finish. "Prince," he said. "Diana Prince. We… she and I… we work together. She helped me get this notebook here. From Maru's lab…"

Steve reached inside his coat and pulled out the notebook, which he presented to Sir Patrick. The man accepted it eagerly and began to riffle through it.

"I think the information inside will change the course of the war, sir," Steve added.

Sir Patrick looked from one of the pages to Steve, his brows raised, eyes wide. "'Dr. Poison' herself? My God," He turned to Colonel Darnell. "Shall we assemble the war cabinet so they can tell us more?"

Darnell hesitated, then nodded in agreement.

Steve's relief was palpable, and Diana, content that the situation would surely soon resolve itself, silently thanked Sir Patrick for his intercession.

Inside her laboratory, Dr. Isabel Maru picked up a green metal canister from the hangar floor and carried it over to a small glass chamber on her lab bench. The chamber contained the very latest in British-issue gas masks. Chemical weapons had not been deployed in any war of the modern era, and the English had spent time and money attempting protect themselves against her increasingly lethal gases rather than developing their own. What irony it would be for them to discover that they had completely wasted their resources. If her current calculations were correct, nothing would save them.

She connected the fitting on the top of the canister to one in the side of the chamber, then turned the wheel on the canister's valve.

General Ludendorff's imposing figure filled the space; as regal as a king, he watched with her as the newly created gas hissed into the containment vessel. A virulent mist filled the chamber and enveloped the gas mask.

Let it work.

Maru clenched her hands and held her breath. She hadn't slept in three days. The Fatherland—and the general—were counting on her to perfect an aerosolized weapon so insidiously caustic that there was no defense against it. A weapon that would turn the tide of the war and bring Germany's enemies to their knees. A weapon with her name on it, which would kill millions. She had run the calculations hundreds of times, testing on paper her chemical formula against the molecular structures of the mask's components. But the results of paper tests could be misleading. Sometimes in real life what should have happened didn't, for reasons unforeseen. But with General Ludendorff by her side, success *must* be hers.

As she and the general looked on, the mask began to disintegrate. The glass lenses cracked; the rubber turned brittle; the metal deteriorated. The sequence of events and their severity seemed unchanged from the previous formulation of the gas. Maru had a moment of doubt. How many failures would Ludendorff overlook? How many failures would his superiors overlook? The general's neck was on the block, same as hers.

It's got to work.

Then, *unlike* the previous formulation, the gas continued to eat away at the mask. The glass lenses cracked even more, the straps broke away from their buckles, the rubber turned to black dust, and the chromed metal became bubbling green jelly. She could barely contain her glee. At last, success.

I have earned it.

Dr. Poison imagined the gas deployed on the battlefield, dropped by aircraft, or buried with explosives underground; there would be no escape. It was the ultimate weapon, unstoppable, a work of genius. The caustic effects of the gas didn't stop with the steaming, rotting mask—the containment chamber's glass walls began to show hairline cracks.

Maru reached for the electrical switch on the side of the chamber. She flipped it, igniting a single spark, which caused the highly flammable gas to spectacularly combust in a blinding flash.

Elated, she looked to the general for approval. He was beaming at her with immense pride. She had done it. She had done it. She would help him win this war. Imagining the moment when he informed the Kaiser that she had come through, she giggled.

And his smile, his approval, made it all worth the sleepless nights and the worry.

I'll do even better, she thought. *I'll never quit improving my ultimate weapon. No army on Earth will stop us. The world will be ours.*

He had made a believer out of her.

Alerted to the crucial intelligence Steve had stolen from the Germans, Colonel Phillip Darnell, Sir Patrick Morgan, General Douglas Haig, and the rest of the British war cabinet crowded with Steve and Diana into a small conference room in the War Office. The walls were covered with maps, photos of Ludendorff and Dr. Maru before her face was injured, and photos of the notebook pages. A terrain map was thumbtacked in the center of the assemblage.

Diana stood near the door, watching, listening to the men discussing the implications of the gas Steve had described. After a few minutes she walked over to the section of photographs. She saw gas bombs, a plane like the one she had freed him from, and a large building called a hanger. Now and then one of the men would glance her way. Steve would say things such as, "She's all right. She's with me. I'm vouching for her." She remembered arguing for his freedom in the courtyard outside the throne room. Their positions were somewhat reversed although these men had no equivalent to the Lasso of Hestia to demand the truth from her.

After a time, there was a shift in the room as the men gazed expectantly at Darnell, who had returned. "Cryptographers had no luck," the man said ruefully. "It seems like a mixture of two languages. But they have failed to determine which two languages."

Diana honed in on the photos of Ludendorff, gazing at his intense face, his hawklike eyes, then turned her attention to Maru's notes. She scanned them. *Oh.* Why hadn't anyone mentioned that before?

"Ottoman and Sumerian," she announced.

The men turned to look at her in obvious astonishment. She was a trifled confused.

"Surely someone else in this room knew that," she said, studying their faces.

Rather than being appreciative, General Haig seemed offended by her remark. As if the fact that she was the one to supply the information devalued it.

"Who *is* this woman?" he demanded.

Darnell glared at Steve as if it was a question he too wanted answered. The Amazons would have welcomed more information about the war from any quarter.

"She's my… secretary," Steve said.

Having discovered what that post entailed, Diana was none too pleased. But as before, expediency was the mother of calm.

"And she can understand Ottoman and Sumerian?" General Haig said dubiously.

"She's a very good secretary," Steve assured him. Laughter bubbled around the room.

"See her out," the general said. Steve was just about to point out the obvious—that they needed Diana—when Colonel Darnell did it for him.

"If this woman can read it, sir," the man protested, "we should hear what she has to say."

General Haig seemed to consider the proposition, then nodded in agreement. "Yes, very well."

Steve glanced her way as if he found it embarrassing

that she observed how narrow-minded the men of this world could be.

Diana scanned the pages again. The subject matter was more puzzling to her than that actual translation. "It's a formula... for a new kind gas..."

The men in the room stirred, intent now, giving her their full attention.

"Hydrogen-based, instead of sulfur." She was sounding out the words, interpreting them.

A shudder rippled through the room. The War to End All Wars had seen the modern introduction of many horrors, including the use of poisonous gas four years earlier. The gases had "improved" over time, becoming more lethal, more devastating.

"Gas masks would be useless against hydrogen," Colonel Darnell said.

Diana continued, "The book says they plan to release this gas at... the Front..." Her heart skipped beats. The Front was their destination. Surely this was more proof of Ares's influence.

"When?" Steve cut in anxiously.

She scanned the pages. "It doesn't say."

"Sir," Steve said, "that is the evidence we need. You have to find out where they're making this gas. Burn it to the ground. Destroy it."

"Ludendorff was last seen in Belgium," Darnell said.

"We can't be sending troops into German-occupied Belgium as we are negotiating their surrender," General Haig said dismissively.

Steve was shocked. That was the first he had heard of a possible German surrender and he hadn't dreamed that it lay within the realm of possibility, given how dismissive the War Council had been of Sir Patrick's efforts to discuss an armistice. He took a moment to process that.

Then he realized that even if a peace were struck, that didn't negate the necessity for their side to contain this weapon of mass destruction. The Germans could simply stockpile it until the next time they felt like taking over the world. And there was no guarantee that the Germans would surrender. They hadn't surrendered *yet*. It was vital to humanity that this ultimate weapon be removed as a threat.

"Sir," Steve continued, "I've seen this gas with my own eyes. If it is used it will kill everyone on both sides."

General Haig cut him off. "That's what soldiers do, Captain." His voice was stone cold, his face as expressionless.

Diana was appalled. Sir Patrick gave her an apologetic look, as if asking her to understand the harsh realities of war.

"Send me in," Steve pushed. "With some logistical support. At least give me the chance to take out Ludendorff and his operation out myself."

"Are you insane, Trevor?" Haig snapped back. "I can't introduce rogue elements like this this late in the game."

"But General…" Steve began.

But before he could press his argument, Sir Patrick spoke up. "Now more than ever," he said, "the Armistice is of paramount importance. We must get it negotiated and signed. That is the best way of stopping the war."

No, it is not, Diana thought. *Ares will not allow it.*

"You will do nothing, Captain Trevor," the general declared. "That's an order."

Diana looked to Steve. He knew she was waiting for him to defy the general as she had defied her mother. In her mind, it was the only way to save mankind. He would be sorry to disappoint her.

"Yes, sir," Steve said. "I understand, sir."

Diana's eyes widened. Heat painted her cheeks. She gazed around the room of satisfied men who sat here far from battle and made plans to send others to their doom. Her eyes locked on Steve, who was acquiescing to this monstrous crime with less force than she had once exerted on her mother to miss a day of school.

"*I* don't," she said.

"Diana, I know it's confusing," Steve began.

She squared her shoulders and raised her chin, staring at him as if he were a complete stranger—which he *was*. He was not a hero, as she had assumed. He was a weakling.

"It's not confusing. It's unthinkable," she said.

"I'm sorry," the irritated general bit off. "Who did you say this woman was?"

"She's with me," Steve replied. "With us."

Diana stood her ground. "I am not with you." She directed her ire at General Haig and the others. "You would knowingly sacrifice all those lives, as if they mean less than yours? As if they mean nothing? Where I come from, generals don't hide in their offices like cowards. They fight alongside their soldiers. They die with them on the battlefield."

"Diana, enough," Steve barked. He turned to the general and said, "My apologies, sir."

Diana balled her fists. "You should be ashamed." She turned on them. "All of you should be ashamed."

Shaking with anger, she stormed out of the room and rushed down a flight of marble stairs. She was revolted; she couldn't get out of there fast enough. The depth of Steve's spinelessness sickened her. She would find Ares on her own.

She would find him in this vast, clogged, confusing world—

"Diana, wait!" Steve called to her back.

She wheeled on him, betrayed and furious. "That's your leader?" she said. "How could he say that? Believe that?" She pointed at him. "And you! Was your duty to simply give them a book? You didn't stand your ground. You didn't fight."

"Because there was no chance of changing his mind! Listen to me…"

"This is Ares and he isn't going to allow a negotiation or a surrender. The millions of people you talked about? They will die. My people?"

Steve spoke over her: "We're going anyway!"

She stopped. Took that in. "You mean you were lying?"

He almost smiled. "Diana, I'm a spy. That's what we do."

She narrowed her eyes at him. "How do I know you're not lying to me right now?"

Steve grabbed hold of Diana's lasso, wrapped the end of it around his wrist, and looked into her eyes. The lasso began to glow.

"I'm taking you to the Front," he said. "And we're probably going to die."

Steve seemed surprised at the last part.

Diana shook her head, but she couldn't help a small

smile in return. Still holding on to the lasso, Steve said, "This is a terrible idea…" He let go of the rope. "We're going to need reinforcements."

10

That evening Diana found herself in one of the seedier sections of what was called London's East End. Steve had led her off the main thoroughfare of Commercial Road, down narrow streets poorly lit or not lit at all, past brick tenements and living spaces that could barely be called hovels. A maze of ramshackle, interconnected cottages. It was a wet night and the air smelled foul from the breeze off the river and the privies in the back yards. There were people staggering about, men and women. Some asked for money, dirty hands extended. There were no beggars on Themyscira.

Steve moved with confidence, comfortable in these circumstances. They exited a narrow alleyway and came out facing a weakly lit set of windows and a sign on a hinge over the doorway. Steve had already explained that their rendezvous with colleagues would take place in a public house, a shop that sold liquid refreshments and bites to eat. Looking at the Hangman's Arms, she couldn't imagine a reason that anyone would want to cross the threshold to do either.

But Steve opened the door and ushered her in.

It smelled like a stable and the clientele were all rough types: merchant sailors, dock workers, ex-Army. Scarred. Dirty. Brutal. And they were inebriated. Some were singing loudly and unintelligibly. Others were arguing.

"These are the reinforcements?" Diana said in disbelief.

"Yup," Steve said affectionately.

"Are these even good men?"

"Relatively," Steve replied.

"Relative to what?"

They moved towards a group of khaki-uniformed Army officers who seemed out of place in the shabby pub. One of them, an exotic, dashing man with brown skin, large eyes and heavy, dark eyebrows, was holding court.

"In Africa, gentlemen," he said, "we had no such luxuries…"

The officers laughed and nodded their agreement as Steve and Diana approached.

"But the luxuries we have now," the speaker continued, "it's like we can't stop making money. My uncle the prince and I would keep it all, but we want to extend the opportunity to a few good soldiers…"

"Which prince was that?" Steve said as he grabbed the man's arm. "I need to talk to you, Prince Madras Angora Cashmere…"

The man grimaced at Steve, but turned and smiled at the men around him, as if to say *forgive my rude friend*. He excused himself with a nod to the others.

"You bugger," he said to Steve when they were out of earshot. "I've been greasing those peacocks all night…" He noticed Diana, who had followed after them. "My goodness gracious," he said, brows raised as he gazed at her. "That's a work of art."

"Sameer," Steve said, "this is Diana."

The man smiled broadly at Diana. "Diana, call me 'Sammy,' please."

"Sammy." Amused, she quirked a grin. First Etta Candy and now this man. Steve Trevor kept colorful company.

Shouts and curses made them turn their heads. On the other side of the pub, two men were having an argument that was threatening to boil over.

Steve waved Diana closer, then said, "Sammy's a top undercover man. Can talk the skin off a cat in as many languages as you."

Diana decided to put that claim to the test. She said in Spanish, "He doesn't look that impressive to me."

Sammy replied, also in Spanish, "You do to me. Your eyes, as soft as your smile…"

One for one, then. Diana moved on to Chinese. "And your eyes look like they want something."

"I know Chinese, too, tricky girl," he answered in the same language.

Then in Ancient Greek she said, "But can you recite Socrates in Ancient Greek?"

Sammy looked at her blankly. He had no idea what she'd said. Diana shrugged as if unimpressed. Score three for the Amazon. Sammy was very gracious as he dipped his head, declaring her the victor.

"Oh, you're done," Steve quipped. That settled, he looked around at the raucous crowd. "Where's Charlie?"

Sammy pointed at the two men who had been arguing and who were now fighting with bare knuckles in a corner of the pub. A huge bruiser was beating the stuffing out of a smaller, younger man.

Diana smiled at the bruiser. "At least this Charlie is good with his fists."

"That's not Charlie," Steve said.

The bigger man landed a blow so powerful that it knocked the small fellow off his feet and sent him crashing to the floor. He groaned.

Steve winced and nodded at the man flat on his back. "*That's* Charlie."

The fighters snarled at one another in a variant of English, but Diana could not decipher the slang. When Steve and Sammy started across the room towards the bruiser, the man realized that Charlie had friends and beat a hasty exit.

Charlie nimbly jumped to his feet, surprisingly cheerful after the punishment he'd absorbed. He plopped down at a table, and Diana, Steve, and Sammy joined him. In a matter of seconds, Charlie had full glasses of whiskey in both fists.

"All right, Charlie?" Steve said.

Charlie looked at him adoringly. "Steve, may God put a flower on your head. Good to see you." Then he downed both glasses of whiskey without taking a breath.

"What were you fighting about?" Diana asked.

"I mistook his drink for mine." He grinned and shrugged. "It happens."

Diana looked at Steve and frowned. She was concerned about his choice of reinforcements. A smooth-talking linguist and a brawler?

"This man is no fighter," she said.

"Charlie here's an expert marksman. It means he shoots people," Steve replied.

"From very far away," Sammy drawled.

Charlie reached out and grabbed a drink from the man seated at the table behind them. "They never know what hit 'em," he said merrily .

But Diana saw a darkness behind his polite smile. He was troubled, or was trouble; either way, she didn't like the idea of an undeclared attack upon an enemy.

"How do you know who you kill if you can't see their face?" Diana said.

"I don't. Trust me. It's better that way."

"My aunt warned me about men like you," she said, and thought of Antiope's reminders that battles were rarely waged fairly.

He leered at her. "Ain't the first time I heard that, lassie."

She went on. "You fight without honor."

His smile didn't flicker, but again, she a cloudy expression move across his face. "Don't get paid for honor."

"What's the job, boss?" Sammy said.

Diana kept her counsel, waiting to see how the rest of this meeting played out. Steve took over.

"Two days tops," Steve said. "We need supplies and passage to Belgium…"

"What's the going rate?" Charlie cut in.

"Better be good pay," Sammy teased.

Steve regarded them. "Well, here's the thing. Uh, I told you it's going to be quick. And there's a lot to be gained by this. It's for a great cause. Freedom. Friendship."

"Okay, you have no money," Sammy said.

"No," Steve admitted.

Sammy gazed at Diana and said in French, "All I want right now is a picture of your lovely face."

Diana smiled at him and replied, "You won't need a picture. I'm coming with you."

Sammy's smile faded. "What is this?" he asked Steve.

Steve nodded. "We're dropping her off at the Front."

"*Dropping her off?*" Sammy echoed.

Charlie looked at Diana. "No offense, *chérie*, but I don't wanna get killed helping a wee lassie out of a ditch, you know what I mean?"

Diana let it go. If Charlie was still there when she challenged Ares, he would learn what an Amazon could do.

The door to the pub banged open and the bruiser re-entered, this time with a pistol. The man leaned in to shoot but Diana coolly grabbed his hand and disarmed him. He grunted; holding him by the waist, she flipped him and sent him flying across the pub. He crashed into scattering of empty chairs and tables. His so-called mates abandoned him, rushing out of the pub.

Astonished, Sammy bent down to help Charlie up. He nodded towards Diana and said, "I am both frightened and aroused."

"When aren't you?" Charlie shot back, rubbing his head. He nodded his bemused thanks at Diana as Steve took the gun from her and put it under his messenger bag. The reinforcements regarded her with newfound respect.

The pub door opened again and a flustered Etta rushed in. "There they are," she said, a forced smile on her face.

A familiar-looking man walked in after her.

"Sir Patrick!" Diana exclaimed.

"That's what I was going to mention," Etta said.

Steve, Sammy, and Charlie stood to attention out of

respect. Steve seemed put out with Etta, who must have told Sir Patrick where Steve had planned to meet up with Charlie and Sammy. Etta shrugged apologetically and made a calming *be patient* gesture with her hand.

"Sit, gentlemen," Sir Patrick said. "Please sit."

He pulled up a chair as the others got comfortable. "I assume you're here planning something that's either going to get you court-martialed or killed."

"I assume you're here to stop us," Steve said.

The elderly man shook his head as he took his ease. "No. Not at all. In fact, I was a younger man once and had I been in better health, I'd like to think I would do the same. I think it's a very honorable thing to do. Therefore, I am here to help. Unofficially, of course.'"

Diana smiled. It seemed there were more good men in this world than she had given credit for.

"What's your plan?" Sir Patrick asked.

"If there is another weapons facility, find it and destroy it. Along with Ludendorff and Maru," Steve said.

Sir Patrick nodded solemnly. "The charming Etta will run the mission out of my office to allay suspicion," he said.

"Run the mission, sir?" Etta said, wide-eyed, a little faint.

Sir Patrick slid a fat envelope across the table to Steve. "It's enough for a few days," he told him.

Steve took the envelope. "Thank you, sir."

Sir Patrick waved off Steve's expression of gratitude. "You're very welcome. Take great care, all of you. And good luck."

We may need to make our own luck, Steve thought. Then he caught the pleased expression on Diana's face. *And I think we're up to the task.*

11

Diana and Steve walked under the ornate entry arch of Paddington Station and into a madhouse of random but purposeful motion. She had never seen so many people crammed into an enclosed space. Everyone seemed happy, even jubilant, which struck her as strange given that it was wartime. Men in turbans marched; others rode past them on bicycles, shouting to each other in Punjabi and laughing. Most people were tending stacks of baggage, and some were tending children as well. A small girl bolted from her mother or nanny, and the woman abandoned her luggage to give chase. There were many soldiers in khaki, presumably headed the same place she was: the Front.

Steve took her arm and they walked to a barred gate where a uniformed man checked their tickets, then let them pass. The air was sooty and the platform gritty underfoot. Diana had never seen a train before; their size and construction fascinated her. Steve had told her in America they were sometimes called the "Iron Horse." A horse one rode on the inside instead of the outside.

The platform was lined with travelers; women dressed as healers and factory workers, Steve said. They served as replacements for the men who had gone to war. Most of the crowd were soldiers, but there were also older men and women who Diana assumed were their fathers and mothers. They were saying goodbye to sons bravely going off to war. Here and there, girlfriends were swept up into uniformed boyfriends' arms and passionately kissed. Small dogs were scooped up and hugged goodbye.

Diana smiled as she watched the sweet farewells.

Ahead of them, a man and a young girl who appeared to be his daughter turned away from a quayside stand carrying curious, cone-shaped objects that they licked with delight. The ice cream seller called out for all to sample his wares.

Steve gave her an amused look. "Hungry?"

Diana nodded enthusiastically. She watched as the man handed them two cone-shaped objects topped with a little dome.

"Thank you," she said.

She didn't know how to approach eating it until she watched him lick at the white ball. She daintily touched it with her tongue and her eyes went wide. Cold. Creamy. Sweet. Delicious.

"What do you think?" Steve asked her.

"Wonderful," Diana said.

There was a little wooden step set out in front of their rail car's open door. Steve took her elbow as she climbed up. She didn't need his help, but the pressure of his hand on her arm—the affection—pleased her.

As she glanced back at him something across the

way caught her attention. A little portable stage had been set up and parents and children stood in front of it, mesmerized by a pair of puppets. One male, the other female. The dolls were shrieking and furiously hitting each other with sticks. The audience, young and old, laughed at the display of violence. Diana watched curiously, remembering a little Amazon so many years ago, watching the warriors learning to fight, not to inflict damage for sport or out of anger, but to protect every single person in this railroad station if the need arose. And the need had most certainly arisen.

The train ride was exhilarating. The landscape flashed past Diana's window at rapid speed—hedges and fences, sheep, goats, villages. After the train screeched to a stop at the Dover docks, she, Steve, Charlie and Sammy climbed down to the platform. Engulfed by clouds of steam, they mingled with the hundreds of Allied soldiers who were also disembarking. The new recruits were jubilant, singing "It's a Long Way to Tipperary" as they marched toward the steam ship that would carry them to the Front. Since the team was traveling incognito, they had had to find a different way to get to there.

As they crossed a bridge, Steve checked his watch. "We've got to get a move on," he said. "Chief won't wait."

"Chief?" Diana said.

"Smuggler," Steve explained. "Very reputable."

Diana glanced at the ragtag team Steve had assembled and her stomach tightened into a knot. Charlie was dressed in a kilt, knee socks, an old blue sweater, a battered Army jacket, and side cap. Sammy wore an overcoat with a fleece collar and a straw boater hat. They were not the kind of warriors she had grown up with, the kind she had modeled herself after. She shook her head and said, "A liar, murderer, and now a smuggler? Lovely."

"Careful, I might get offended," Steve said.

"I wasn't referring to you."

"Really? I went undercover and pretended to be something else. I shot people on your beach and I smuggled a notebook to London. Liar, murderer, smuggler." He paused to let that sink in. "Still coming?"

She acquiesced and let him lead her away from the soldiers, down a different path—narrower, muddier. It wound away from the station to another set of docks. A white ship with a huge red cross on the side was disgorging its passengers. Diana recognized the healers' uniforms—they were the same as the ones on the train. Except that they were soiled and stained with blood. And the healers themselves looked exhausted and wretched as they helped wounded young soldiers down the gangway to the dock. Some of the young men were carried on litters because they were too injured to walk, even with help. Some had faces completely covered with bandages. Some were missing limbs.

"It's awful," Diana murmured, hurting for these fallen warriors.

"That's why we're here," Steve said soberly.

Steve put his hand on her shoulder as she took in the horror, the despair, and the waste until she could look no longer. *This is what must stop*, she told herself. *This is why I must stop it*. She took a firm grip on Steve's arm and they turned away from the hospital ship and towards the next dock.

They walked down the pier to a sixty-foot boat with a wooden pilothouse set high above the deck. There were bumpers on the sides and at the bow. It was flying a blue, yellow, and red flag. It was not the flag she had seen everywhere in London. The same colors were repeated on the vessel's smoke stack that was puffing black exhaust.

"Romanian tug boat," Steve said as they climbed aboard. "The favorite nation of spies and smugglers. Won't draw attention when we dock on the other side of the Channel."

Almost immediately the lone crewman cast off the mooring lines and the boat began to back away from the pier. The captain, a bearded man in a cloth cap, did not greet them or introduce himself. He seemed only interested in getting out of the harbor as quickly as he could. Once he turned the bow into the wind, an afternoon that was merely chilly became downright cold. The sky threatened rain. As strange as the vessel was, as strange as her new companions were, as dark as her future looked, Diana found comfort in the familiar motion and the smell of the sea.

Steve did not wake her up the next morning; she woke him, and Sammy, and Charlie. The crewman exited the tiny galley and handed them each a steaming mug of tea. They went up on deck to watch the sunrise and enjoy their spartan breakfast. The weather had calmed overnight but the skies were still gray and threatening.

After the tug was moored to the dock, Steve paid the captain out of the money Sir Patrick had given him. Diana brought up the rear as the team set off across the docks. A troopship was tied up on the pier opposite. Diana saw horses being unloaded. War horses. Some of the animals wore gas masks. It was a bizarre and disturbing sight; the implication chilled her to the bone. On Themyscira, she had been taught to revere the land and its animals, which had been placed under the protection of the Amazons by Zeus.

"The gas will kill everyone… everything," she said.

Steve nodded in agreement.

"What kind of weapon kills innocents?" she asked, a rhetorical question. She was not naïve, but all this was new territory to her in so many ways.

"In this war?" Steve said. "Every kind."

Charlie took out a tattered map, referred to it, then said, "We have a bit of walk ahead of us. Nice day for it, though."

But the blue sky became a grim counterpoint to the horrors surrounding the quartet as they slogged through a sepia world of browns—mud-covered soldiers and fleeing civilians. Thin, exhausted mothers carrying clinging children, their wide, frightened eyes cutting Diana to the quick. This should not be the kind of world that any child saw. Men carrying bundles of possessions. Desperation, fear, flight. Men whipped a poor horse stuck in a muddy pond. Violently, urgently. The distressed creature whickered in protest; it couldn't budge. Other horses were similarly maltreated, by men equally skittish.

"These animals. Why are they hurting them?" Diana protested.

"Because they need to move," Charlie offered.

"This is not the way. I could help them." Diana prepared to do just that, but Charlie shook his head.

"There's no time. Come on, woman."

They passed a maimed soldier lying in the mud, crying out in pain. "That man. He's wounded."

"There's nothing we can do about it," Sammy said. "We must keep moving."

The pervasiveness of the horrors all around them tore at her. Every instinct to stop, to help, warred with the urgency of finding Ares. Once he was dead, this hideous hell would cease to be. But in the meantime, she was an Amazon, sworn to protect all mankind, and these people needed her desperately. Each step she took past the suffering was bitter and hollow. The Great War had already claimed the lives of millions, and the hungry maw of death was eager to devour millions more.

The torturous trek led them into an oak forest; as the last of the daylight faded, they came upon a campfire near the crossing of two dirt roads. A man wearing a large, broad-brimmed hat, a buckskin jacket, and a choker of bone and beads tended a campfire.

"You're late," the man said as he rose to his feet. His rifle was decorated with brass studs in a series of unusual designs. He picked up a piece of wood from a small pile and threw it on the fire.

"Cowboy sneak attack, Chief," Steve said.

The man embraced Steve, and nodded a greeting to Charlie and Sammy.

"It's good to see you," Sammy said.

"Aye," Charlie added.

The Chief turned to Diana. "Who is this?" he said. "*Niitangio, Napi.*"

Diana understood. She replied in English. "I am Diana."

Her response in his language surprised and pleased him. "Where did you find her?"

"She found me," Steve replied.

"I plucked him from the sea," Diana began.

Steve waved for her to stop. "It's a long story," he interjected. Sensing a need for discretion, Diana complied.

Beside the campfire, a tent had been pitched. In the firelight Diana saw a pile of packages of various sizes wrapped in oilcloth and several guns leaning up against them. One of the crates was open and it was neatly filled with tall brown bottles.

"What are those?" Diana asked.

Steve looked at the stuff and did a running tally. "British tea for the Germans." He showed her a packet. "German beer for the British. Edgar Rice Burroughs novels for both sides."

"And guns," Charlie said. He walked over to the stockpile and picked up a gun. It had a small metal tube on top, what in their private conversations Steve had referred to as an "Aldis Pattern three-power, telescopic sight." She recognized the gun from his description: it was a British Lee–Enfield Model P14. Charlie shouldered the sniper weapon and looked through the sight, then gave the stock a big wet kiss, like a father reunited with a long lost child.

While Diana watched, the others helped themselves to guns. It pleased her that she could recognize them too. Sammy grabbed a Lee–Enfield Mark VII, .303 caliber. And Steve, the American, picked up an American gun, a Winchester 12-gauge repeating shotgun. Thanks to Steve, she also knew their magazine capacities and effective firing ranges.

Steve, Charlie, and Sammy helped themselves to bottles of beer from the crate. They stood in a circle with the man known as the Chief, holding up the bottles.

"May we get what we want," Charlie said.

"May we get what we need," Steve added.

"But may we never get what we deserve," Sammy said.

"Bang," they said, clinking the bottles together.

In less than ten minutes Charlie was snoring curled up by the fire. Steve and Sammy joined him a short while later. The Chief opened some cans of food and heated them in the fire.

There was an ominous rumbling in the distance. The sky was overcast, no visible stars, but it wasn't stormy.

"Strange thunder," Diana said.

"German seventy-sevens," the Chief said. "Guns. Big ones." He pointed in the direction of the rumbling sounds. "That's the Front out there. The evening hate."

The Front. So they were close. Diana's heartbeat picked up. Soon she would battle Ares. And she would defeat him with the Godkiller. This misery would all end.

He handed her a can of beans and a spoon. She tried a bite and frowned. It tasted like bits of chalk in a disgustingly sweet sauce. She set the can aside. Not all the food here was good.

"So," she said to the Chief, who was counting a thick wad of paper money bills, "who do you fight for?"

He stuffed the money into his pocket. "I don't fight," he said.

"You're here for the profit, then?"

"No better place to be."

"Nowhere better to be than a war you don't take a side in?"

"I have nowhere else and no side left. The last war took everything from my people. We have nothing left. At least here, I'm free."

"Who took that from your people?"

The Chief gave her a puzzled look, as if questioning her seriousness, as if the answer was so obvious. But she really didn't know, and he seemed to understand that. He motioned to Steve, who slept peacefully. "*His* people…"

Before Diana could follow up with more questions, Charlie stirred in his sleep. First he began to murmur, then whimper, then his limbs jerked as if he was having a terrible nightmare. She watched him with growing concern until he suddenly cried out, eyes popping wide open, mouth gaping. The cry echoed through the forest and awakened Steve and Sammy, who sat up.

Diana reached out to Charlie compassionately, gathering him up. "You're safe," she said. "Are you okay?"

He shrugged her away. "Get off me, woman. Stop making a fuss."

He got up and helped himself to another beer. Diana noticed that his hand was shaking as he tipped the bottle back. She sat back down.

"He sees ghosts," the Chief said. Diana could imagine that he must, fighting without honor as he had.

Steve got up and fetched her his coat. "You're going to get cold. Here."

She began to explain that she didn't feel the cold as he died. Amazons were impervious. "No, I'm…"

And then she realized that he was extending her a kindness. The gesture, like his hand on her elbow helping her into the train car, were evidence of his thoughtfulness. The sign of affection warmed her far more than the coat.

"Don't worry about Charlie," he told her softly. "He doesn't mean anything by it."

This war. This terrible war.

12

Ludendorff fumed as he returned the salutes of a pair of sentries guarding a fortified bunker deep in German-occupied Belgium. It had been a long drive and he had been delayed several times. On one level that could be amusing, given who he was. But he was not amused.

Pushing open the door, he entered the bunker. The ceiling was low, and the members of the War Council stirred as he made his appearance.

"You were absent at the Council meeting, General," *Generalfeldmarschall* von Hindenburg said by way of greeting.

With concealed fury, Ludendorff glared at him. "I see you've begun negotiating the terms of the Armistice."

"On the Kaiser's behalf," von Hindenburg said pointedly.

"On your insistence." Ludendorff addressed the rest of the council. "We can easily win this war still, if only you have faith."

As if to forbid any discussion, von Hindenburg rose to his feet and said, "We don't. There are shortages of food, medicine, ammunition. Every hour we delay costs thousands of German lives."

"One attack," Ludendorff said with emphasis, "and the war is ours. As we speak, my chemist and her team are…"

The general field marshal cut him off with a wave of his hand. "We stand against you and your *witch*, Ludendorff! Enough!" Von Hindenburg gathered his dignity and continued in a more moderate tone. "Twenty-four hours from now this war will end. It is over."

Ludendorff looked von Hindenburg in the eye, then the other generals one by one. *I gave you a chance,* he told them silently. *You have sealed your fates with your cowardice.*

"It is over for you. For all of you," he said.

With that he turned on his heels and exited the bunker. Outside the door, he gave the signal for Dr. Maru to proceed. She opened the door a crack and tossed in a canister of gas. Ludendorff stopped her from shutting the door. Leaning in as the metal cylinder rolled along the wooden floor and came to rest under the table at von Hindenburg's feet, he threw in a gas mask. He and Dr. Maru watched the eyes of the general field marshal and the members of the War Council follow the arc of the mask to the floor. Then he slammed the door and put his back against it, holding it shut.

The canister exploded with a dull thump. Poison gas billowed into the small space and sounds of coughing and fighting came from inside the bunker.

"The mask won't help," Dr. Maru reminded him.

"Yes, but they don't know that," Ludendorff said. They both laughed.

Instead of rushing the door to get out, the choking men were wasting precious seconds battling over a mask that would save no one. The irony was delicious.

Perhaps finally realizing that, the men trapped inside threw themselves at the door, but they could not budge it. Their screams of pain and betrayal grew more and more faint, until all that could be heard was the steady hissing of the canister.

Dr. Maru watched through a window, transfixed by the effect of her creation. The beautiful biology of it, the chemical reactions that to her were nothing short of miraculous. This, her first field test, had produced precisely the intended result. She laughed with delight.

Ludendorff reached into the pocket of his great coat and took out a small glass capsule of an altogether different sort of gas—another of her inventions. He cracked it open between his thumbs and deeply inhaled the contents. The effect was a blinding rush of energy and power. It made his veins swell and pulsate, and for an instant his eyes bulged as if they would pop from their sockets. He had come to crave the sensation, and this blend was even more potent than the last one. She had not shirked in her duty to him.

If only I had possessed this elixir long ago, he thought. Then he grabbed her by the arm and pulled her away, though she was loath to leave until she had confirmed a one-hundred-per-cent kill rate "Let's go. It's time to stage our demonstration for the Kaiser," he said.

The sun was just breaking over the tree tops as Diana and the team advanced down a narrow unpaved road. The Chief was in the lead, his eyes searching the ground ahead. "You'll want to walk behind me," he told Diana.

"And why is that?" she said, challenging him.

The Chief stopped and gestured for Charlie to hand him his beer bottle—Charlie and Sammy were having beer for breakfast. Charlie shook his head, clutching the bottle to his chest. Sammy handed his over without protest. The Chief then hurled the bottle in a high arc. It landed about a hundred feet ahead of them, bounced once, then bounced again. When it hit the ground a second time, there was a loud explosion and a puff of smoke.

Everyone ducked as bits of hot metal sang overhead and clipped small branches off the trees on both sides of the road.

"That's why," Steve said. He went on to explain that the Germans had put land mines on many of the roads, this to keep their forces from being flanked by the English and their allies.

Diana fell into line behind him. She nodded at the Chief, who had once again resumed walking. "He's not frightened of death?" she asked.

"Chief says he's had a vision," Sammy said. "He doesn't die in this war. He goes to Russia and drinks vodka with the Tsar."

Diana glanced at Steve and shook her head. "And you think *I'm* crazy."

Steve cracked a smile.

The hell of war.

Ochre clouds, rusted farm tools, broken bricks in piles.

The sound of Diana's heartbeats melded into the clatter of gunfire, the boom of cannon, and the flat crack of distant explosions. The muddy field they were traversing offered scant cover, and bullets whined close overhead. Diana kept her eyes on Steve's boot soles as he trudged ahead of her. As they advanced in a daisy chain, the team shambled through a sloppy furrow in the muck.

The gunfire wasn't aimed at them. Both sides were dispiritedly firing back and forth at each other across a wasteland of devastation at least a quarter-mile wide. The desiccated tree trunks gave testament to the fact that this once had been part of a forest. Occasionally there would be a scream as a soldier was hit, in the deep trenches cut into the plundered, exhausted earth.

"What is this?" Diana asked Steve.

"You wanted me to take you to the war. This is it. Front lines," he said grimly.

They climbed down a ladder into another world. The bottom of the trench was clogged with muddy-faced Tommies—British soldiers. Some were so covered that their eyeballs looked unnaturally white, their mouths and tongues red as raspberries. Charlie and Sammy joined them. Flurries of bullets nipped at the sandbags along the top of the ditch, and shells screamed down from high overhead, exploding in the muddy field so close that they made gobs of blown-up mud pour down on them. It was difficult to hear—and to think—because of the repeated, violent concussions. A red sign read: DO NOT STAND ABOUT HERE. EVEN IF YOU ARE NOT HIT SOMEONE ELSE WILL BE.

"Where are the Germans?" she asked.

Charlie hooked a thumb towards the source of all the incoming small arms and shellfire. "Couple hundred yards that way. In a trench just like this one."

The Chief waved for them to follow him. Diana and the others began to move through a seemingly endless narrow passage carved deep into the earth. Clumps of soldiers, obviously exhausted, sat on crates or leaned against sand bags. The wounded were laid out on stretchers, the lucky few wrapped in soggy blankets.

One of the soldiers brightened as he saw them approach. "Chief!" he exclaimed. He shouted the news down the trench. "Oi! Chief's back!"

A pair of officers rushed up to greet him. One of them said, "Chief, welcome back. In the nick of time!"

The Chief reached into his coat's deep pockets and began passing out packs of cigarettes, matches, and candy to the grateful soldiers. Despite his introduction to Diana as a smuggler, he waved off their offers of money. Gentleness and sympathy softened his features as he gave all he could to the warriors, some of whom accepted his kindnesses with tearful eyes. Diana's heart filled with compassion; this suffering and privation must end.

"All right. Let's move," Steve said.

Then Diana heard what sounded like a woman weeping.

A young mother holding her daughter rushed forward, beseeching the Chief in French. Standing by, Steve clearly didn't understand what was being said, but Diana did.

"The Germans took everything—homes, food—and the ones who couldn't escape they took as slaves," the distraught mother reported.

"Where did this happen?" Diana asked her.

The woman pointed beyond the trench, into the indeterminate distance.

Diana turned to Steve. "We need to help these people."

Steve looked across no man's land and shook his head. "We need to stay on mission."

The Chief agreed with Steve. "And there's no safe crossing for a least a day away."

Charlie took his flask from under his jacket and knocked back a quick swig. "Then what are we waiting for?" he said as he screwed back the top.

"We cannot leave without helping them. These people are dying," Diana said. "They've nothing to eat. And in the village—*enslaved*, she said. Women. Children."

Steve faced her. "This is No Man's Land, Diana, which means no man can cross it. This battalion has been here for more than a year and they barely gained an inch because on the other side there is a bunch of Germans pointing machine guns at every square inch of this place. This is not something you can cross. It's not possible."

Diana gave his argument no credence. "So what? So we do nothing?"

"No. We are doing something," he reminded her. "We just can't save everyone in this war. This is not what we came to do." His expression was earnest. She knew it cost him to say it—that he had had to harden his heart in order to press forward with his mission. But her heart was not hard, and she did not believe that the heart of an Amazon could become so. She had been created to bring harmony to the world—not to turn her back on it. So be it.

Diana turned away from Steve to prepare herself for battle. When she faced him again, her hair streamed free over her shoulders and she had put on Antiope's headband. Beneath her cloak her shield was strapped to her back, and her lasso hung from the right side of her waist.

"No, but it's what I'm going to do." She moved past the astounded team, climbing up the trench ladder. As she ascended, she dropped her cloak, revealing the armor she had taken from the armory on Themyscira—a crimson breastplate of the same metal as her tiara, a golden waistband, her short Greek warrior skirt in blue, gauntlets, metal foot guards and shin guards, and leggings that came up past her knees. Steve, the Chief, Charlie, Sammy, and the Tommies in the trench looked at her in astonishment—and awe.

She reached the muddy verge and readied herself for action, finding the core of strength inside herself.

The power.

"Diana!" Steve cried.

She stepped onto the battlefield and surveyed the ground ahead. Her armor gleamed against the colorless stretch of No Man's Land—the Princess of Themyscira, defender of the people, majestic, magnificent. Driven by compassion and her commitment to justice to save the villagers of this town.

On high alert, she strode down the space separating the trenches—a quiet, lifeless plain of mud and shell craters, empty except for the coils of barbed wire attached to wooden crosses that stretched across the hell-blasted landscape. They were meant to ensnare soldiers as they tried to advance and make them easy targets for the waiting machine guns. With each step Diana took, her foot squished into the ooze.

From the German trench opposite there was a quick

flash. A soldier had fired at her. She tracked the bullet as it crossed No Man's Land at a crawl, and when it came close enough for her to see it spinning, she swatted it aside with her bracelet. The bullet zinged off at a steep angle and it was only then, what seemed like an eternity later, that the sound of the distant shot caught up to the action. There was another flash from the same spot. Another block as the projectile slammed into her bracelet.

From the trench behind her she heard Charlie exclaim, "How the hell'd she do that?"

Diana continued to stride across the battlefield; at every step she met and deflected new bullets. The flashes from the opposing trench were constant and spread out in a line thirty yards wide. The Germans thought they had an easy target; they thought they had a chance to take her down. But they were wrong.

With each impact Diana learned more about absorbing the force directed at her. She walked as the fusillade ricocheted off her gauntlets. What they sent at her, deflected back in a torrent that stitched along the sandbags on the trench's rim. Her pace began to quicken, a fast walk, then a trot, then she started to *run*. Over the rattle of gunshots, Diana heard Steve's shout.

"She's taking all their fire!" he said. "Let's go!"

Without hesitation, Steve led the others over the top, leaving the stupefied British soldiers behind. The Germans were determined to hit Diana; she raced for the German lines, making the staccato *tack-tack-tack* stream of bullets spark off her bracelets. Nothing could stop her, nothing could even slow her. She ran faster and faster, straight into the teeth of the storm of lead.

Out of her line of sight, panicking German soldiers,

unsure who or what she was, lifted a mortar into position. As their comrades fired shot after shot until their gun barrels glowed red, the mortar team rained high explosive warheads down on the lone sprinting figure.

To the others on the battlefield who were seeing and hearing events in real time, the mortar shells screamed in a high soprano as they fell on their target. To Diana, they moaned in a baleful baritone. She used her shield to bat them away, and they exploded in the mud on either side of her.

She was within two hundred feet of the German trench when a heavy machine gun opened fire on her from a fortified nest on her right. She blocked the barrage of bullets with her shield, ducking her head behind it and driving forward with her shoulder.

A second machine gun opened fire from the other side. She continued to advance, but the sheer force of all the bullets striking her shield slowed her to a crawl, her feet slipping in the mud. She dropped to one knee, protected by her shield from the hail of bullets, and glanced behind her.

Steve and his team were crossing the field, closing the gap. Steve rushed up and took cover in parallel a few hundred yards away from her. They exchanged glances, comrades in arms, defenders of the people. He had a warrior's heart, like hers.

Steve shouldered his repeating shotgun and fired. He pumped the slide and fired again and again. Buckshot swept across the front of the German trench, knocking the soldiers back. She could hear the pellets *ping!* as they slapped against steel helmets and the *smack!* as they struck flesh and bone. Steve's shotgun blasts gave her a bit of breathing room, but the machine guns still had her pinned, pouring lead against the front of her shield, trying to find a weak point and exploit it.

Charlie used his sniper rifle to lay down covering fire as the Chief tossed Sammy a hand grenade. Sammy pulled the pin, picked his target, released the safety, and pitched the bomb overhand at the machine gun nest on Diana's right. It was a long throw, but perfectly aimed and timed. The Mills bomb landed next to the MG 08 and before the soldiers manning it could move, it exploded in a bright flash and puff of gray smoke. The blast knocked the weapon off its base, and sent the Germans flying in all directions.

The Allied forces rose out of the trenches, shooting as they charged after Diana, Steve, Sammy, the Chief, and Charlie, freed from years of fruitless struggle. The second machine gun continued to unleash sustained fire on Diana, hammering her shield, but it lacked the force to hold her down. She rose from her crouch and began to run, taking the full brunt of the automatic fire as she picked up more and more speed, closing on the enemy position. When she was fifty feet away she jumped high into the air, leapfrogging over the sandbag fortifications. The gunner kept firing—at empty space. The German soldiers' upturned faces as she descended were full of shock and horror. The shock was only beginning. She landed in the middle of the machine gun nest. Spinning in a blur, Diana used her shield like a bludgeon, smashing it down on the machine gun, breaking it in two.

"Steve, let's go!" she cried, leaping back out of the trench.

On either side of her, the allies poured into the enemy

trench. The din of gunfire was one-sided. The Germans fell into a frantic retreat down the narrow passage, abandoning their wounded comrades and in some cases their own weapons, trying to avoid being overrun by the mass of British troops.

Diana turned toward the village of Veld, which lay on the far side of enemy lines, beyond a low hedge row. Leaving the Tommies to clear the area of combatants and hold ground, Diana took off through the cold, slanting rain and the sucking black mud, heading straight for the village. Steve, the Chief, Sammy, and Charlie raced after her.

Diana advanced to the edge of the little town. The buildings that faced them were pocked with bullet and cannon holes. A lot of the windows were missing glass and boarded up. The cobblestone streets and the sidewalks were covered with mud and the debris of battle: pieces of masonry blown off the facades, broken glass, scraps of wood, and shell casings from thousands of spent bullets. The villagers had vanished; there was no one left to clear it away.

As she advanced, gunfire roared at her from second-story windows on the far side of the street and from ground-floor doorways on that side. Bullets gnawed holes in the brick walls behind her and sparked off the cobblestones at her booted feet.

She raced towards the gunfire, sword at her side, shield on her back. It seemed that every bullet fired at her made her stronger, quicker, more agile. Her power was growing and it felt amazing, as if there was no end to it, as if she was tapping into something immeasurably vast, as if she was a conduit for an elemental force.

She didn't bother slapping the incoming bullets

aside—she dodged them. Moving at tremendous speed, she outran the blast effects of the grenade explosions. She traversed the entire gauntlet of small arms and grenade fire without receiving so much as a scratch and yet the street was choked with swirling clouds of cordite smoke.

Diana took off running to build up speed, then sprang ten feet in the air. She hit the side of a building and vaulted off of it. Using the full power of her legs, she jumped even higher. High enough to crash through a second-story window in the building opposite where most of the concentrated gunfire was coming from. She landed in a crouch in a stripped room with a rough wooden floor, in the middle of a group of armed German soldiers. Before they could raise and aim their rifles at her, she kicked a heavy table that screeched across the floor and slammed into two of the soldiers, pinning them against the wall.

Unable to believe their own eyes, the terrified Germans began firing at her at close range. She ducked under the slow-moving bullets, some of which sailed past and hit the soldiers behind her. Their bodies fell to the floor.

A soldier snapped his rifle across her back; it shattered and she kicked him through the window. She moved so fast that sparks flew from the soles of her boots. She skidded across the floor on her knees and slammed a soldier with her shield, flipping and twirling high into the air, an Amazon in full-strength combat mode. Sword and shield, fists and legs, she threw kicks and punches to clear the rooms. She swept the feet out from under a soldier and before he, too, hit the ground she swung her shield, batting him like a ball through the broken window.

Diana was like a whirlwind in their midst, a force of nature that could not be stopped. The surviving soldiers backed away with empty hands, then broke for the door.

Diana heard the receding bootfalls of the men who had escaped. She raced out of the room and down a narrow hallway. The Germans were still shouting at each other. Then they suddenly went silent. But she had already honed in on the source of the sound. It lay behind a heavy wooden door.

No doubt they were ready for her on the other side. Or thought they were.

Bracing her feet, she threw herself shield-first at the door and shattered it like a cannon shot, sending splinters and sawdust flying around her as she burst through the doorway. The room full of Germans attacked her as one, using their steel-shod rifle butts as clubs.

They didn't realize that she, not they, had the advantage, but that quickly became all too evident. They were too slow and too weak to keep up with her. She swung her shield left and right, using the edge to crush the sides of their helmets. The impacts snapped their heads back and sent them toppling to the floor. They tried to raise their rifles against her, but, with fists and feet, she beat them to the floor before they could get off a single shot.

And when she finished, there were only two people left standing in the room.

Running full tilt, she hit the last soldier in the chest with her shoulder, driving him backwards. The impact's momentum carried them both across the room and through the glass of a big window. For a second they were soaring, then she landed on top on the roof one level below and raced from rooftop to rooftop toward the center of the town.

As she ran, she looked for Steve and the others, but

they were not yet there. But she was confronted with an unexpected arrival: an armored tank, roaring toward her on its steel treads, maneuvering its 57 mm cannon to bear. Diana jumped down from the high rooftop like it was stair step. She lowered her head and headed toward the tank.

The tank shot; Diana deflected the cannon fire with her shield, then dropped it as she charged the tank. And it yielded. The bonds of gravity, the inertia of its thirty-six tons, none of that mattered. She flipped the tank. It went flying end over end across the town square, and as it did, pieces of it sailed into the air; the steel treads snapped off. The soldiers who had stood behind it were suddenly without cover themselves.

At the moment, she became aware that Steve and the team had arrived, and were seizing the opportunity to advance. They poured fire on the Germans who, instead of standing and fighting, ran for the square's nearest exit. The ones caught flat-footed absorbed multiple hits and fell where they stood. Steve waved for the team to follow him. They chased the soldiers down the street, firing on the run.

Steve sent the others to free the prisoners and burst into the square beside Diana. She was surrounded by German soldiers who were firing at her from all sides. She blocked their bullets with her bracelets, moving in blur, spinning, ducking.

He pulled the pins on a pair of grenades. A handful of Germans was shooting at Diana from behind a crumpled armored car. Steve underhanded one of the grenades, skipping it over the pavement and under the car. When it exploded, the soldiers were trapped between the side of car and the wall of the building.

The blast stunned the other soldiers in the square. They stopped firing and looked at the armored car, which had burst into flames. The Germans firing from behind the fountain stood up to get a better view. Steve lobbed the second grenade in a low arc that ended in the middle of the ruined fountain. When it exploded it sent not only shrapnel flying, but pieces of masonry that cut down the soldiers like a scythe.

Diana smiled at him as they moved in unison.

More soldiers poured into the square. One of them started climbing up the ladder to the village bell tower. Steve fired at him, but he was out of the shotgun's effective range. Diana charged into the German reinforcements, snatching them off their feet and throwing them like rag dolls, bouncing them off the sides of the buildings, off the sidewalk.

Steve looked over his shoulder; a German was aiming a rifle at him and others were closing in. The soldier's finger was already curled around the trigger. Before he could fire, Diana was on him. She tore the gun from his hands and, swinging it by the barrel, broke the butt stock over the top of his helmet, putting a deep dent in the steel pot, driving the man into the ground like a tent stake. Whipping out her lasso, she snared one of the others by the foot, jerked him off his feet, then used his body as a sledge hammer, swinging him around and around, and smashing him into his slack-jawed comrades.

Covering the town square, they fought together, moving in concert, each reinforcing and supporting the other. Diana unleashed her lasso, using it to wrangle the soldiers, spinning them, as Steve laid down covering fire. Lessons they had learned together on the beach of Themyscira and in the trenches of No Man's Land—combining strengths, adopting each other's strategy and tactics—proved the advantage as they fought for the freedom of the village.

Fierce volleys barked as more Germans entered the square and once again Diana deflected bullets with her bracelets. She and Steve worked side by side, she blocking, he shooting. He saw the rest of the team hurrying into the square to back them up, taking position along a row of storefronts. Suddenly Diana jumped behind Steve and thrust up her hand. The bracelet knocked aside a shot that came from above them. That was intended for his head.

Steve looked up and pointed. "Bell tower," he said. He could see the sniper at the top of the tower. No one in the square was safe.

"Charlie?" he said, motioning for the man across the square to take the shot.

Charlie dropped the safety on his rifle and leaned against the building's wall, peering through his telescopic sight. His hands were shaking and he couldn't seem to catch his breath. Sweat began to pour down the sides of his face. Seconds passed. More seconds. He could feel Sammy staring at him. He put the crosshairs on the German silhouette crouched below the bell.

But he couldn't squeeze the trigger. He was frozen in place, captured by his own fears as surely as if he had been taken prisoner.

The soldier's weapon flashed again, and the round hit the sidewalk in front of him. Then bullets were flying down at Sammy and the Chief. All three were pinned where they stood.

"You don't miss," Sammy said.

"Bloody scope," Charlie said. "Lens is cracked."

When Sammy tried to get a look at it, Charlie covered it with his hand. It was not the scope, of course. It was him. He had cracked.

Diana watched Steve rise from cover, then duck back as a bullet from the sniper zipped by his head. There was no way to return fire from their position.

Diana looked up at the tower, gauging the distance between herself and the target. Frustrated, she told him, "It's too high."

Then Steve spotted the tank door, which had blown off. He remembered Antiope's heroic leap on the beach. He said to the team, "Follow me. Give me some cover. When I say 'go' lift hard."

They did as he asked, and the four of them raised up the sheet of metal as Steve called, "Diana! Shield!"

She understood at once. With a running start, she thrust her feet against the angled surface as they hefted it hard and she soared into the air. She rocketed up, and farther up, and crashed into the bell tower. It seemed to hover in space for a second, and then it tumbled down in huge waves of bricks and mortar, metal and glass, utterly demolished.

A roar went up from directly below her. The townspeople had emerged from hiding and gathered to cheer her heroic victory and their restored freedom. Diana looked down at them from the great height. She could see Steve looking up at her with awe.

Thank you, Antiope, she thought. *What I did today, I dedicate to you.*

The jubilant townspeople surrounded their liberators, shaking Diana's hand, thanking the group for saving their lives. One of the villagers was a photographer and he insisted in broken English that he be allowed to photograph the liberators of Veld—*pour la postérité.*

"You must stand very still, very still," he admonished them. Diana, Steve, Charlie, Sammy, and the Chief posed standing on the rubble at the edge of the square. Steve looked at Diana, but turned his head toward the camera before the flash powder went off. His expression hinted at something more than admiration.

"Thank you for this *honneur,*" the man said.

After the photo was taken, Diana walked with Sammy to survey the damage the battle had caused. She looked back at Charlie, his head hanging low, clearly shaken, his mind turned inward. He fumbled with the screw top of his flask, then dropped it.

"For all his talk of murdering people from afar," Diana said to Sammy, "your shooter can't shoot."

"Not everyone gets to be who they want to be all the time. Me, I wanted to be an actor, not a soldier. But I'm the wrong color. Everyone is fighting their own battles," he concluded. "Just like you are fighting yours."

Diana considered, then noticed the Chief standing with a small group of Belgians who had taken cover in the allied trench, including the young mother and her daughter. All of them looked ragged, sleep-deprived, and starving, but hopeful. The Chief dispensed bread and cheese to all with a big grin on his face. Again, the so-called "smuggler" was the benefactor. She was touched by the man's generosity. She remembered her dismay at the pub when she had first met Sammy and Charlie, brawling and lying. Her opinion of them had changed dramatically.

Across the square another cheer went up from the villagers, who were busying themselves in preparation for a party to celebrate their heroes and their liberation. The square was being swept and cleaned, evidence of the battle removed, and men were stringing up party lights and setting out tables.

13

As the villagers of Veld prepared for a celebration, Steve used the phone in the village's one and only inn to report in to Etta Candy.

"Veld," he said, reporting their position. "Tiny village. It's probably not even on the…"

Steve looked up and Diana in the entryway and held out the handset so that she could hear too, giving her a quick tutorial by gesturing to his ear. Diana's grin was quick and sharp. No phones, of course, on Themyscira.

"Found it," Etta announced the other end.

"Have you found Ludendorff's operation?" Steve asked her.

"Not yet," Etta told them, "but we've located him. And lucky you, he's only a few miles away—at German High Command."

"German High Command?" he repeated.

"Intel reports Ludendorff is hosting a gala—a last hurrah before the Germans sign the Armistice. The Kaiser himself will be there. As will Dr. Maru."

Steve began mentally sketching out a scenario.

"Actually, that gala's perfect cover…"

Sir Patrick's voice came over the line. "Captain Trevor, you are not, under any circumstances, to attend that gala tomorrow night. We cannot risk jeopardizing the Armistice."

Diana lowered the handset and told Steve in an undervoice, "You shouldn't be worried about upsetting the peace accord. Ares would never let that happen."

Steve motioned to her to please stop talking about Ares.

Then Diana flinched, struck by a realization. Why hadn't it dawned on her before? Her Amazon blood blazed super-hot as the thrill of the hunt coursed through her. Her heart thundered and her body demanded battle. Her quarry lay within her reach. In her mind, she saw their story unfolding in her mother's beautiful paneled book. The final chase, the victory. Diana with her sword, her defeated quarry at her feet.

She wished with all her heart that her mother could be with her to witness her triumph. That Diana could prove to her that she had made the right choice—that both of them had. Diana for leaving, and Hippolyta for giving Diana her blessing.

Her emotion must have shown on her face because Steve asked, "What is it?"

"Of course," Diana said, "it makes complete sense. Ares developed a weapon, the worst ever devised."

"Ares? You mean Ludendorff."

She looked Steve in the eye. "No. I mean Ares. Ludendorff is Ares."

It was difficult to decipher the expression on Steve's face, but to her it translated as the same thunderstruck revelation.

"Steve?" Sir Patrick said.

Steve returned his attention to the conversation on the phone. "Sir, this is our chance to find the gas and learn how Ludendorff plans on delivering it. Maybe our only chance. Our last chance."

"I forbid it. Do you hear me?"

Diana watched Steve closely, but this time she was confident that he would do the right thing. He had pretended once before to do as Sir Patrick had wished, and he was pretending now.

Sure enough, Steve paused as if weighing a decision. Then he said, "I'm sorry, sir, you're breaking up."

"Steve? Are you there?" the man protested.

Steve quietly hung up the phone. Diana wanted to embrace him. Instead she forced herself to breathe deeply. She had a battle to prepare for.

A peace to make.

Back in London, Etta disconnected the call as Sir Patrick looked on.

"How likely is he to respect my wishes?" he asked her.

Etta shrugged. "Not very likely, to be honest," she replied.

That night, villagers sat at tables in the town square of Veld, which were scattered with platters of sausages, cheese, and bread—the hoarded food of the Germans plus their own meager stores brought out for the celebration. Though scarce by Themysciran standards, it was clearly a banquet to the starved villagers, freely shared. Their gaunt but relieved faces were illuminated by tea lights, and despite their exhaustion, they wore smiles and tapped their toes to the music. Joy at their deliverance glowed in their tired eyes.

Inside the building marked "Café Bar Buvette" with its cheery striped awnings, a man sat at a large instrument made of wood. It took Diana only a second to realize with delight that this was a *piano*. He pushed his fingers downward and music flowed. He was *tickling the ivories*. She smiled as she made the connection. How strange it was, to possess vast vocabularies in languages she had never heard spoken by anyone but her own people, and now to encounter them where they were used. There were so many unexpected details and nuances. Everything was so different from home—harsher, darker, crueler— but alleviated with kindness and warmth, even in the midst of a catastrophic war.

A deep pang caught her as her mother's face rose in her mind. *You are my greatest love*, she had told Diana. *And my greatest sorrow.*

If you could have seen me today, I would have been your greatest pride, Diana thought, as voices in the café lifted in song. *What we did today was possible because of you. And Antiope, who made me the fighter I am. Humanity could use the help of all the Amazons. This world is aching. This world is in such danger.* Danger, and terror; and yet, here, tonight, men and women smiled and danced. They shrugged away the perils and lived.

As she scanned the clusters of people at the tables, a pair of children chased each other, squealing with delight. As with the baby in London, she was mesmerized. She had never played with another child. "You know nothing about the world," Hippolyta had told her, and that had been true. And yet, the Queen of the Amazons had allowed her to leave everything she had known behind. Perhaps like Diana, she had heard the wind and the waves whispering into Diana's ear: *This is your destiny. Your quest. You must do this.*

Steve joined her at the edge of the crowd. There were greater victories to be won, at higher prices. This war, this endless war—she could chip at the edges of it, save those she could, but until she brought down Ares, pain and suffering would wash over humanity like the dark, dirty water of the London seaway, receding only briefly to leave treasures on the beach. Tonight was one such treasure.

Sammy approached with two large glass steins of a beverage whose scent was like the yellowing hillsides of Themyscira in summer.

At home the Amazons had spent centuries perfecting their painting skills, creating pottery that was as finely wrought as their armor, swords, and shields. In London, there had been such a disparity in the quality of all objects, from clothing to tankards to dwellings. Some people staggered down the dirty London streets in rags. Others strutted proudly in the choking finery Diana had tried on for Etta. On Themyscira, some Amazons were higher-ranking than others, but a sister would never allow another sister to go without.

With a jovial smile and his maroon fez cocked at a jaunty angle, the dark-skinned man held out the tankards.

"Drinks later, Sammy," Steve said. "I need you to rustle me up a German uniform."

"Already done," Sammy proclaimed.

Diana wondered how he had accomplished that,

but Steve was obviously relieved.

"There's nothing we can do until tomorrow," Sammy went on. "You said it yourself, Steve." Giving him a pointed look, Sammy strolled off.

Steve raised the tankard to his lips and sipped. Diana did too, but was caught off guard by the burst of flavor on her tongue. There was no honey in this mead. She had been surrounded by this drink at the pub back in London, but this was her first actual taste.

"It has hints of different flavors, if you look for them," he said.

Indeed, she thought, and mentally replayed the day. Hopelessness, death, and destruction, and then battle, and life, and hope. The mandate of the Amazons on its way to fulfillment.

I will free this world, she thought.

"You did this," Steve murmured, indicating the celebration, the smiles, the freedom.

Diana corrected him. "We did." The piano song lilted softly in her ear.

"You have dancing on 'Paradise Island?'" he asked her.

She reflected a moment, then said, "There is. These people are just... swaying."

Steve said, "Okay, if you're going to be fighting the God of War, I may as well teach you how to dance." A beat, and then he added, "Probably without the gun."

He removed his holster and gun and set them down and said, "Madame, if you would?" He extended his hand and she took it.

She said, "Well, if I'm going to a gala, I'll need to know how to—"

"You're not going to the gala," he cut in.

She cocked her head. "Of course I am. Why wouldn't I?"

"Because you don't know how to dance, for one thing," he said.

She indicated the other dancers. "I would argue that *they* don't know how to dance," she countered.

"All right. Give me your hand like so and I'm going to put my arm around you like so and we just, what did you call it? Sway."

Skin on skin, warm. He put his arm around her waist and tingles played in the small of her back. When she had bent over him the day that she had saved his life—and he, hers—she had been intrigued by him, yet unafraid. She was still unafraid, but subtle emotions entwined with untried sensations. The palette of life at home had not contained such light as that which danced in his eyes.

Things have shifted between us, she realized. *There's been a change, somehow.*

Around her, lights and joy sparkled, the heady nimbus that came with victory. Fighting side-by-side had been a different sort of dance.

"You're awfully close."

"That's what it's all about," he drawled.

"I see."

Then the music changed. A male voice rose sweetly over the melody, soaring with emotion. It was lyrical, transporting, and it was Charlie, the troubled assassin of men. He had taken over the piano, and it was he who was singing. *These men, with their strains and threads of goodness.* Ares did not command them fully; some, she supposed, had escaped his influence entirely. Was the man who faced her, who held her, one of them?

Sammy and Chief joined the people crowding around Charlie, smiling, laughing, grateful for life and good company, for a moment of pure pleasure. The song rose in pitch, plucking at her heartstrings. Steve's hand at her back grazed her like a brazier. They swayed, embracing each other.

Charlie sang:

"I'll walk beside you through the world today
While dreams and songs and flowers bless your way.
I'll look into your eyes and hold you hand
I'll walk beside you through the golden land."

"I haven't heard him sing in years," Steve said.

What appeared to be a white flower petal fluttered down from the dark sky. Another, and another; they sprinkled Steve's hair. She held out her palm, catching a few, and sniffed. Not flower petals at all. They transformed into water drops in her hand.

"It's a snowfall," Steve explained. "Touch it."

She knew the word. But to *experience* snow? She laughed. "It's magical."

He blinked, then looked up, and nodded. "It is, isn't it."

They danced. The snow drifted down. Children, songs, hope.

"Is this what people do when there are no wars to fight?" she murmured.

He spoke against her ear. "This and other things."

"What things?" she urged.

He paused. "I don't know. They… make breakfast."

They make their morning meal, she translated. "What else?" she asked.

"Read the newspaper. Go to work." He paused again. "They... get married. Maybe have babies, grow old together. I guess." He sounded wistful, a bit out of his depth.

"What is it like?" She watched the falling snow as it melted on the shoulder of his coat. The warmth of him surrounded her.

"No idea," he confessed.

He pulled her in closer. She looked deep into his eyes and her chest hitched. They were dancing in more than one way, that much was clear.

Glistening snow swirled down.

Beneath the gentle snowfall they walked back to the inn. Then up the well-worn stairs, which creaked like the wood of a ship. Almost floating, Steve opened the door and Diana walked into the room. A fire flickered in the grate. He followed in, then reached for the doorknob to leave. Paused.

She was looking at him intently. Expectantly. She was inviting him.

He shut the door behind himself and faced her. The firelight played over the hollows of her face, her hair, her eyes. So beautiful.

She reached up with both hands to run her fingers through his damp hair. She pulled him to her, mouth to mouth, in the most perfect, gentle kiss. Amazon princess, soldier. Champions. This was not about that. This was about love, and goodness. They would not wait for this evil war to be over. This was their time.

Their pact was made.

14

A new day. Pines silvered with frost; a wash of crimson across the heavens. The holes left by grief and longing, filled with fresh happiness.

The team was milling near a copse of trees—skittish Charlie in his Scots cap; Sammy, debonair in his fez; the Chief in his Native American garb, patient and at ease. Diana smiled in greeting as she approached. Steve was dressed in a German uniform that fit him well. Her blood stirred. Then she took note of five horses, one for each of them. They were good animals, although perhaps not as muscular as the ones back on the island. Farmers' horses, not warriors' mounts.

"The villagers gave them to us," Sammy said.

"A gracious gift," the Chief added.

"They called us heroes." Sammy was abashed.

She knew they hadn't come with Steve to be heroes. They had come for money, maybe adventure. But she had seen them in the field. They had risked everything in battle.

"You *are*," she said.

All three of them looked startled, and she realized that the power of her conviction had forged errant wish into solid truth. Even Charlie forced a smile at her, struggling to agree.

"Hey, folks," Steve said tentatively, "I'm fully aware that I said this job was two days and a deal is a deal—"

He was giving them permission to walk away. The Chief scoffed and said, "You would get lost without us."

"Yeah," Sammy put in, "we know Diana's capable of looking after herself, but I'm worried *you* wouldn't make it."

Steve grimaced at the affectionate jibes. "There's no more money."

Sammy patted his horse. "We've been paid enough."

The Chief nodded, but Charlie hesitated. He was shaky, like the young men in the mire of the trenches in No Man's Land. It was not lack of courage that dogged him, but lack of belief in himself. The world had shaken him off his feet. This war was not like the ancient Greek wars she had studied, which had been filled with honor and a clear code of conduct. They had fought that way until the Peloponnesian War, when, under the patronage of Ares, the Spartans had broken those barriers. This war was like that one, with terrifying new weapons and shifting alliances, its cruelty to civilians and utter destruction of the land. This war did not bring valor to its warriors; it brought nightmares to all.

"You'd be better off without me," Charlie said.

Diana gave him a kind smile, willing his spirit to find some peace in the chaos. "No Charlie, but who will sing for us?" Reminding him of days gone by when he did sing.

He brightened as Sammy groaned and said, "Ah! Don't encourage him!"

But Charlie was encouraged, and he did sing as the team mounted up and left the grateful village. He sang loudly, fiercely, like a proud *bacchante*. Their band moved on through the dappled sunshine. Moved forward toward their shared destiny: to end this.

And as Diana put her heels gently to her nickering horse, she was touched by the surprising depths of goodness that she continued to discover within these battle-hardened men.

Steve lost the thread of his conversation when Diana came back into view on her horse. She was trailing slightly behind, gazing around herself at the enormous oak trees. His breath caught. This war must end; they must survive it. He wanted to show her the good world he was fighting for—a world he had barely remembered until she had come along.

"You must think I was born yesterday," Charlie exclaimed, and it took Steve a moment to catch back up to the reference: Charlie was reacting to the story Steve had just told about his commandeered Fokker going down just inside the protective barrier around Themyscira, and how Diana had come to his rescue. And about why she had left her home behind to come with him.

"I know it sounds crazy," Steve replied, "but it's true."

"Wait," Sammy said eagerly, "there's a whole island of

women like her? And not a single man among them?"
He was practically drooling. "How do we get there?"

Steve just smiled.

Sammy cocked a brow. "And she thinks *Ludendorff* is Ares? The God of War?"

"And only by killing him the war will end?" Charlie added.

Sammy peered over his shoulder at Diana, then shrugged his shoulders. "You saw what she did out there. The way she charged that machine gun nest. The way she took out that tower. Maybe it's true."

The Chief nodded thoughtfully, but Charlie shook his head and narrowed his eyes at Steve.

"You don't really believe all this rubbish, do you?"

Yes, he had seen her fighting, whirling like a tornado, doing things not humanly possible; he had been forced to answer questions when that lasso had tightened around his chest. Yes, he had been to the Land of the Amazons. But he had also seen poison gas dissolve leather and metal. In his world there were machines that flew, and electricity. You could receive inoculations that made you invincible to rabies and smallpox. Those things would appear magical to someone like Diana. They were not the work of a God, but science: the work of man. Maybe there was something in the water on Themyscira that gave the women extra strength. The Lasso of Hestia could be made from a fiber that contained a native truth serum…

Yes…

He was being ridiculous. Diana possessed something far greater than "extra strength." Yet now, looking at the disbelief on the faces of his friends, certainty faded. They were talking about the Ancient Greek God of War. As far as Steve was concerned, Ludendorff was the Devil incarnate. He and Dr. Maru, a sadistic, heartless scientist who had marred her own beauty to advance the cause. But a God?

He studied Diana, who was riding up to meet them. He believed in her. In the big picture, their interests coincided. Ludendorff and Maru must be stopped. It wouldn't end war on Earth; it wouldn't end this war. But the world would be better for it, and they would be one step closer to peace. This time. And that would be enough for him. But for her?

I would do anything to give her what she wanted, he thought, as the sunlight played on her dark hair. His horse chuffed as she drew near, tall and straight on her mount.

Through the dappled sun and shadow, deeper into the woods.

Hours of riding drifted by, the inexorable *clip clop, clip clop* of the horses, oaks and larks, a breeze: the calm before the storm. Steve's men grew quiet—even Charlie—and he knew they were mentally preparing for the next step in their plan.

Then they reached the field of play: the location of tonight's gala. It was all coming down to this.

Through the trunks of the ancient trees he made out the walls of a stone castle that vaguely resembled the fortress-like headquarters of German High Command back in Berlin. Berlin had been a city frozen in ice, the people frightened off the streets. An ominous portent of what life would be like if the Germans won this war.

Steve had blended in like a chameleon, infiltrated the highest circles, and stolen military secrets. His German was excellent; he had passed easily. Other spies had not been as fortunate…

Signaling a halt, he scrutinized the imposing building through his field glasses. A long line of chauffeured limousines paraded across along a road past a guard. Men in uniforms and civilians in party clothes were arriving for the celebration of the Armistice. Would Ludendorff and Dr. Poison intervene? Steve plotted out a dozen possible scenarios as he continued his recon. He needed to stay focused and calm. When he had gone down in the waters of Themyscira, his only thought was that he had unfinished business—getting Maru's notebook to London. But now, aware of Diana's nearness, he had an unfinished *life*. And he wanted to share it with her.

Don't think about that now, he told himself sternly.

This stopping point would serve as their base of operations; as with all other missions, it would be their rendezvous point if they were separated. That was, if they could figure out how to conduct their mission…

The men dismounted and crouched low, surveying the facility through the trees. Diana stood in plain view until Steve said gently, "Diana. Diana. Hiding. Hiding."

She moved into the shadows.

"How the hell are we going to get in to that?" he asked the others.

"The way in is through the gate," the Chief replied.

Charlie scoffed. "'The way in is through the gate.' Is that supposed to be some ancient tribal wisdom? Gee, thanks, Chief."

Without another word, Chief disappeared into the

dark forest. Off to assess the situation. Good. Charlie raised a telescope, and through his field glasses Steve saw what so interested the Scot: several guards stood at the entry gate, but only one guarded the building's entrance.

"If you could get through the gate," Charlie ventured, "I see only a couple of guards at the door to distract."

Steve frowned. "It won't look at all suspicious when I come sauntering out of the woods on foot."

There was a beat of silence and then Diana said, "I could get in."

Steve furrowed his brow. She looked at him steadily. "You're not going in. It's too—dangerous."

"Too dangerous?" she echoed, as if he were joking.

"Yes. Too dangerous," he said emphatically. "And you're too distracting." That was probably the truer of the two reasons. She could probably tear down the entire castle without breaking a sweat. "I'll go in there and follow them to where they're working on the gas, or better yet, find out where it is."

"I am coming with you," she announced.

Man, is she stubborn.

He gestured to her Amazonian clothing, her headband, her bracelets, her cleated boots. "No, you're not. What you're wearing doesn't exactly qualify as 'undercover.'"

"I don't know, I'd say she was pretty under cover," Sammy quipped, but Charlie was the only one who laughed.

Steve had to make sure she understood. That she believed him. That she wouldn't do something rash. "There's no way to get you in. Let me scout it and report back."

She flared. "But as long as he's still alive—"

"You can't go into German High Command and kill anyone! You have to trust me, Diana." He was practically begging—and he wasn't used to that. But her line of reasoning was suicidal: Kill Ares—Ludendorff—and everyone would immediately embrace each other as brothers. What would be more likely to happen would be death by firing squad for the entire team. Amazons died too if they took a bullet. He had witnessed that firsthand on the beach.

As she opened her mouth to argue, an open-air Rolls Royce limousine purred through the trees towards them. It was a gleaming black beauty, and although the Chief looked very much at home in the driver's seat, his outfit—domed hat, bead choker, fringed leather vest—didn't exactly shout "Chauffeur." He braked to a stop and gazed placidly at Steve.

"Where did that come from?" Steve asked in astonishment.

"Field over there is full of them," the Chief deadpanned.

Sammy was agog. "Can I drive it? Lemme drive it. I'll be your chauffeur!"

Steve smiled. The first domino—the limousine—had just been placed on the board. Sammy was the second domino. The Chief got out and Sammy climbed behind the steering wheel. He was a perfect choice, completely believable. With his swarthy complexion and command of languages, he could easily pass as a Turk or Arab—German allies in the Kaiser's war.

He gave Diana a look, mentally exhorting her to really, really listen to him. Then he slipped into the backseat of the Rolls and Sammy put the pedal to the metal, weaving his way through the forest. It was a smooth ride; Steve cast his mind back to the flood of innocent people fleeing the war on foot. He was here for them.

After they reached the road, Sammy glided to the long drive flanked by trees and pulled to the back of the line of other limousines waiting for admittance to the grounds. The guard at the gates was taking his time checking the papers of the people in the car at the head of the queue.

Steve's adrenaline began to pump.

Charlie stood beside the Chief, watching as Sammy's Rolls pulled in behind a parade of idling luxury cars. Motorized vehicles of any sort were far out of the economic range of the likes of him, particularly in wartime. A good used bicycle was more his speed. Although his dear old dad didn't think much of them: "Wear out your legs giving your arse a ride," he liked to say.

He was grateful to Diana for encouraging him to stick around. Drink and nightmares had been taking their toll. But last night, he had slept better than he had in years. It was good to be back with the fellows, counting on teamwork, making a difference for a worthy cause. There was none worthier than freedom.

"We should scout the area in case we need to beat a hasty retreat," Charlie said.

The Chief nodded. "What do you think, Diana?"

There was no answer. They both turned to look behind them. "Uh-oh," Charlie muttered, his stomach dropping to his knobby knees.

So much for teamwork.

The bloody Amazon was nowhere in sight.

* * *

Curtain rising, Steve thought, chewing anxiously on the end of a pipe he had stashed among his things in his messenger bag, still with him despite all the craziness. He used the pipe on occasion for disguises. Seated in the back of the limousine, he stared at the back of Sammy's head, which was wrapped up in a tea towel, also from the bag, in a good approximation of a turban. Making do with the resources at hand was part and parcel of the espionage game. Sammy's lifelong ambition to be an actor had come in handy on more than one occasion in the past. The way Steve figured it, he himself had the simpler role, but not the easier task—he had to sit in the back and stay alert while feigning nonchalance. He well understood Diana's impulse to *do* something.

They inched along, creeping closer and closer to the gate. Steve breathed deeply and surveyed his surroundings. The old trees lining the drive reminded him of Washington, D.C. The castle itself was distinctly Old World, a paean to fairytales adorned with gabled roofs and tall towers. The stylishly dressed women walking up the grand entry staircase could have stepped out of Parisian fashion magazines. The German elite appeared to be as hungry for peace as the peasants of Veld—though for different motives, he assumed. The poor wanted to survive; the wealthy, to profit.

The limousine managed another inch forward. Then another. They were within a car's length of the checkpoint. He fought the impulse to drum his fingers on his knee.

Then Sammy cleared his throat and said anxiously, "Steve, they have *invitations.*"

Sure enough, as the car in front of them pulled up to

the gate, a gloved hand extended from the driver's side dangling a piece of paper. The guard took it and pored over it as if he were studying for an exam. He actually held it up to the light to check the watermark. Then he handed it back.

Steve's spy brain began to consider solution. *If we could find a piece of paper, scribble on it, get it wet… maybe they wouldn't look at it that closely?* A few things were missing: paper, water, a pen, and time. Could they pull out of line? No. There was no room, and it would look suspicious.

Well, so much for stealth. Time to move on to bluster.

"Don't worry. Play it cool. You got this," Steve assured Sammy.

They had no choice but to approach the gate. One of the guards held out his hand. Sammy clasped it with both of his and shook it, hard.

"*Dhanyavaad, sahib,*" he chirruped. "The colonel and I wish many blessings and all manner of other things to fall upon your head —"

Steve took his cue. "And *your* head's empty!" he growled. "He wants my invitation, you idiot!"

Sammy dipped and bowed, groveling as one did before their German overlords, and kissed the German's hand. Astonished and repulsed, the guard attempted to pull it away. Sammy held on for dear life.

"I must apologize a thousand *thousand* times, my masters, for I made the most horrible, the most unforgiveable mistake. I lost the colonel's invitation."

Steve made a show of checking his watch and then he let Sammy have it. In perfect German, he shouted, "What! Are you saying we drove all the way through the mud and rain only for you to lose my invitation!"

"I am a snail!" Sammy wailed. "No, a bug. No, the *dung* of a bug!"

Bluster won the day; the bewildered and uncomfortable guards shooed them on, eager not to make a scene when it was obvious that these two had been master and servant for quite some time and it would cause far less havoc to be rid of them.

Sammy grinned at Steve and drawled, "Blessings be upon us."

Steve smiled back, but as they drove on, his smile faded when he spotted a squad of German soldiers setting rows of seats a distance from the palatial building, as if for a viewing or a parade. *What is this?* Unease prickled the back of his neck.

By then they had reached the front of the chateau. Sammy played the chauffeur, leaping out to open Steve's door, giving him a deep, servile bow.

Steve raised a brow at him. Sammy smirked, pressed his palms together, and bowed deeply again. Soon he was bowing and blessing the seemingly endless line of arriving Germans, who turned away from him with apparent distaste. "Prince Cashmere" finally had a part that was made to be overplayed. Steve found that both ironic and amusing. He flashed a grin. Then he put on his game face and joined the party.

From the protection of the trees, Diana contemplated her options to get inside the castle. Then she noticed a female party guest striding toward the entrance in a striking blue gown. Diana moved along the bank of shadow below the building's windows and melted into the trees as the woman approached. When she was ten feet away, Diana stepped out of concealment and into her path. The woman froze, shocked by the sudden approach. Then her eyes widened and her brows lifted as she took in Diana in her long cloak, greaves, and armored shoes.

"What are *you* supposed to be?" she demanded haughtily.

Ignoring the woman's ire, Diana moved even closer, sizing her up. *Close in height,* she confirmed. She kept one eye on her target, the other on possibility of witnesses. As the woman tried to move past her, Diana backed up and maintained the close interval.

"What are you doing?" the woman snarled, stopping again.

Her indignation was cut short by Diana's quick, powerful hand chop to her neck, a blow that landed in the tight space where her neck met her throat. The woman made a soft *ooof* sound—an involuntary expulsion of breath—and her eyes rolled back in her head.

In the shadows Diana laid her down on her back and quickly undressed her, deftly unzipping and unfastening. No longer was she bewildered by the complex clothing of the women of this world. She recalled her visit to Selfridges, and the kindness and stretched patience of Etta Candy, and smiled to herself. If, one day, tales were told about her adventures in the world of men, they must include Etta, who was brave in a very unique way.

The deep blue, floor-length sheath fit perfectly over Diana's armor. Having now seen that the women wore their hair up especially when attired for special occasions, she removed the jeweled hairpins from the woman's hair, and plaited and twisted her own locks. She had spent hours playing with her mother's hair when she was a little girl, braiding and unbraiding it while Hippolyta sang lullabies or retold the old story about how she had made Diana from clay and begged Zeus to breathe life into her. It took her very little time to achieve an appropriate hairstyle. The long dress hid her boots; she hid her bracelets inside the folds.

After taking the woman's invitation, Diana wrapped the woman in her cloak. The Godkiller she kept, hesitating for only a moment before she slid it down the back of her dress, assuming correctly that the ornamental hilt would look like part of the gown—at least for as long as it took her to get inside and find her quarry.

She practiced yanking it out and thrusting it in a single, blindingly fast move—dealing an unexpected and instantly fatal blow. Her blood sang. The Godkiller came to life in her hand. She had been born to wield it, of that she was certain.

Replacing it between her shoulder blades and down the length of her spine, she walked around the front of the chateau. Her chin raised high, she regally strode up the stone stairs to the entrance. Her heart skipped beats as she handed over the invitation and swept inside. Heads turned her way, following her. Her vibrant blue dress stood out in the sea of gowns. She relaxed her facial muscles, then smiled with her eyes, projecting calm, ease. But inside her breast a warrior's heart thumped, and her every gliding step was the supple, precise movement of a lioness advancing on her prey.

* * *

It doesn't matter if they stare at me, Dr. Maru told herself. It was perhaps the twentieth time she had reminded herself that night as perfectly coifed women swirled around their male companions like so many pampered Persian cats. Her purpose in life was not to dazzle with something as shallow and fleeting as physical beauty. It was to win glory for the Fatherland through scientific inquiry, and tonight would be the culmination of her life's work, and the reward for all her suffering. She had lost what looks she had once had in a lab experiment. Beneath the scars the memory of the searing pain still lingered. Her drive to succeed in a field dominated by men had given her the strength to move past it, and to excel. Let them glitter in the jewels and silks they acquired through their men. She had medals and commendations from High Command.

Tonight she and General Ludendorff would prove to the Kaiser that, contrary to the wishes of von Hindenburg, he must not negotiate an armistice with any foreign power. Peace must come off the German table. Tonight her weapon would change the course of history. For that achievement, she would have paid any price.

15

Dr. Maru watched the guests walking down the receiving line, many of them flushed with the excitement of meeting the Kaiser. That excitement became muted when they came face to face with her. She wished she were back in the lab, double-checking everything, making sure all was ready, and that the bodies of the men she and Ludendorff had gassed had been properly disposed of.

A number of people asked her when von Hindenburg was going to arrive. The Armistice was his to celebrate, and the party would be incomplete until he appeared. General Ludendorff had been so wise to dispose of von Hindenberg and his fellow weaklings. She had prepared a response for the question; each she shrugged as if there was nothing to worry about and replied that she had heard he had been "delayed" but would arrive soon. Very soon.

But that answer would not satisfy them for long. Even the Kaiser was beginning to shift uneasily and scan the throng for that familiar face. More and more guests were beginning to look at watches and to murmur among themselves.

The next time she came abreast of Ludendorff, she said, "They're starting to ask where von Hindenburg and the others are."

"Soon it won't matter," he replied, his attention elsewhere. That was true. But as the lag leading up to their demonstration dragged out, she began to lose her poise. Everything must work flawlessly. It was one thing to run an experiment in the lab. But this would be the first real test of her brainchild. And if it didn't work—

It will work, she told herself. *You have tested and retested every single component. The trajectory is correctly calibrated. And you know what the gas will do.*

Chandeliers and candles gleamed. There was so much glitter and glamor, men in uniforms and formalwear dancing with ladies in all the latest fashions, clusters murmuring and laughing and sampling the fine Belgian delicacies including chocolates. She hadn't even had time to arrange her hair, find a more flattering dress.

Irrelevant, she thought, and she moved to a fireplace, seeking composure as she gazed into the flames and waited.

Here goes nothing, Steve thought, as he plucked two glass of champagne off the tray of a passing waiter and approached the woman he had come to regard as a mad scientist. How else to explain why she took such glee in the horrors she inflicted on her victims?

"Excuse me," he said to Dr. Maru, who appeared to be lost in thought as she gazed into the flames of a cheery fire. He held up the glasses, his opening play.

"I don't drink." She blinked and wrinkled her forehead. "Have we met?"

This was a gamble. If she recognized him, he was in big trouble. It was unfortunate that he hadn't been able to smuggle in more of the team. His thoughts flickered with an image of Diana, whom Maru and Ludendorff had never seen. No. Diana wouldn't have contented herself with espionage. She would move directly into action—attacking Ludendorff in the middle of the party, and never mind the consequences. Steve had done the right thing… but what if Dr. Maru realized he was the spy who had stolen the notebook?

"No, but I've been watching you," he replied, injecting warmth into his voice as he regarded the monstrous woman. He forced himself to focus on her eyes and not look down at the eerie flesh-colored plates. "Following your career. I mean, you're Dr. Isabel Maru, the most talented chemist in the German Army. I'm a fan."

He briefly shifted his gaze to Ludendorff, and she caught him. He covered, thinking fast. "I hope I'm not crossing a line. I hear you and General Ludendorff are *very close.*"

Her back visibly stiffened. The uncovered side of her mouth drew into a thin line.

"We *work* well together, yes," she replied.

That was his cue to turn on the charm. He smiled flirtatiously. "I'm sure he provides a great deal of support for you and your work, but having someone like me *behind* you…" He let that double entendre work its way to her. "…I could provide a lot *more.*"

His words did not have the desired effect. There was no pink in her exposed cheek, no eye blink, nothing to suggest that his flattery was welcome. But she did regard him more closely.

"And *who* are you?" she said.

He realized that the standard rules of seduction did not apply in this case. She knew she wasn't beautiful or desirable. He reasoned that compliments meant to turn her head had to be directed at a different target.

"A man who would show you the *appreciation* a genius like yourself deserves," he said.

Dr. Maru stared into the fire. There. A tiny smile gleamed from the mobile half of her mouth. Yes, focusing on her intelligence. That had hit home. In a big way. He definitely had her attention now.

"I love fire, don't you?" he asked silkily. "It's like a living act of entropy. The ultimate weapon of destruction reminding us that, in the end, everything eventually returns to the ash it once came from. There's something... reassuring about it."

From her reaction, he could tell that she liked that analogy. She turned to him and again stared deeply into his eyes. He fought to keep his expression warm and sexy, but he felt as if he were facing down a cobra. Having seen firsthand what she was capable of, it was difficult not to flinch at her slightest move.

"I see all that in your eyes," he added, doubling down. What did the Brits say? *In for a penny, in for a pound...*

Yes, yes, she was buying it. She needed to be appreciated for her accomplishments by a man smart enough to know *she* was smart. Maybe he could get her to show off.

"Perhaps you could tell me what you're working on? I hear it is extraordinary."

She parted the right side of her lips, preparing to speak. At last, the answers he needed. He remained calm… outwardly.

And then… out of the corner of his eye…

Oh. My. God.

He stopped breathing. Everything stopped. Diana stood at the top of the stairs. She glowed in a deep blue gown; her head was held high, regal; her hair was swept up, revealing the long column of her neck. *No, no,* he thought, as she turned her head and her expression shifted to a predatory scan of the room, undetectable to anyone who didn't know her field techniques.

But he did.

As Diana turned a bit more, he caught sight of the crossguard, grip, and pommel of the Godkiller, which she had slid down the back of her gown. To the untrained eye, it looked like part of the decoration of the dress. She was prepared to kill Ludendorff here and now, but if she did, it wouldn't stop the Germans from using their new weapon. It would only get the team killed.

And it looked like Maru was about to tell him everything they needed to know. Once they had the details, they could run their own covert operation. They didn't need to come out in the open like this, on a suicide mission.

"I appreciate your interest in my work," Maru said, "but I am loyal to General Ludendorff. Besides, now I see your attention is directed elsewhere." She laughed sharply, and Steve understood that she had busted him for staring at Diana.

Then Diana looked straight at Ludendorff. Their gazes locked. Steve could see she was studying him intently. He saw a flicker of emotion in her intense concentration.

Was she now uncertain that Ludendorff was Ares? Would that stay her hand and keep the mission intact?

What is she going to do?

Diana walked towards the being who was her destiny. Every footfall echoed in her head. She heard her heartbeat and—so strangely—the ticking of Steve's watch. Was she right that this was Ares? From a distance the general looked all too human. She sharpened her senses, staring at him with a warrior's eyes. Should she feel something emanating from him? Could she sense the depth of his power? How did one know when one was in the presence of a God—the God who had killed all the Gods?

I feel nothing unusual. What of him? Could he tell who she was? That she was his nemesis, the Amazon who had come to bring peace to humankind?

Her heart was thundering as she closed the gap. Everything depended on this moment. Stealth was one of her gifts. The defeat of her foe was another. She could almost feel the Godkiller leaping into her hand, and then the smooth, well-aimed thrust. The world's suffering would end. The chains of evil would fall to dust.

If she was right.

Then he grabbed her. She prepared to fight back—

—and as he put his arm around her, he began to sway.

To dance.

With her.

His hungry look… his arrogance. She studied him, searching for proof positive that he was the God of War. Locked in his arms, she could not reach for the

Godkiller without interrupting the charade of manners he had forced her into. She had not expected that. She wondered if he could hear her thundering heartbeat, the pump of her blood. The blade of the Godkiller pressed against her spine. She sent a silent thank you to Steve— wherever he was in this place—for teaching her how to dance in the approved way. She could keep up this masquerade for as long as was necessary. She stayed focused on him as party guests milled and danced past gleaming candelabras and glittering jewels, oil paintings and magnificent statues. He was imposing and regal, clearly at home amid the splendor.

"Enjoying the party?" Ludendorff asked her.

Her eyes narrowed slightly. "I confess I'm not sure what we're celebrating tonight."

"A German victory, of course," he said with relish.

"'Victory?'" she echoed. "When I hear peace is so close?"

He smiled. "'Peace is only an armistice in an endless war.'"

It was a famous quotation. Her heart turned over in her chest. She understood what he was saying. And whose words he was using to say them:

"Thucydides," she replied, referring to the Greek general who had written about the long, terrible war between the Spartans and the Greeks. Mnemosyne, Diana's last tutor, had forced her to memorize long passages of his work. She had told Diana that Thucydides was one of Hippolyta's favorites—and by that she meant both the work and the man.

"You know your Ancient Greeks," he said. "They understood that War is a *God*. A God that requires human sacrifice."

Her pulse quickened. Who would say such a thing

besides Ares himself? She willed herself to remain calm. To dance. To bide her time until the proper moment.

"And in exchange, war gives man purpose, meaning," he continued. "A chance to rise above his petty, mortal little self and be noble, better than he is." He raised his chin. His eyes glinted. He believed what he was saying absolutely. It was his code.

There was no question now. *This is Ares.* A strange quiet came over her. She felt as if she had been born to do this. To take her sword and end him. She would let nothing, neither man nor God, stop her from fulfilling her destiny.

She became aware that he was waiting for her to speak. Her nerve endings were sparking; her blood boiled.

"Only one of the many Gods believed in that… and he was wrong," she replied. She wanted desperately to grab her sword, but he was still holding her hand in the dance position. She knew that when she made her move she had to be unencumbered. There could be no way for him to escape.

"You know nothing about the Gods," he said, taking a deep breath. And in that moment, the horns on a statue directly behind him seemed to protrude from Ludendorff's own head. He looked like Ares in her mother's triptych, gazing down with malice at the human race.

It is he. I am in Ares's arms. I am inches from his heart, and I have the Godkiller. It is time.

But a soldier approached and hovered doggedly behind him as they danced. She gauged her ability to strike with the man so close. She must not be interfered with. "General?" the man said.

Ludendorff looked over his shoulder, then checked his watch. He let go of Diana and retreated a step, conferring with the man.

Then he turned back to Diana. "Enjoy the fireworks," he said.

I must do it now. The shouts of Gods and Amazons chorused in her heart as she reached over her back again for the grip of her sword.

Before she could touch it, Steve moved between them, facing her. Smoothly, he pulled her away from the general, taking her hand, turning her—and starting to dance with her, as Ludendorff had done.

"What are you doing? Out of my way," she demanded. It was barely a dance, more like a wrestling match.

He locked gazes with her. His mouth was set. "Diana, look at me. If you kill Ludendorff before we find the gas, we won't be able to stop anything."

After all this time, did he still not grasp the truth? She could not conceal her impatience and frustration. "*It won't matter,*" she said, putting emphasis on every syllable. "I will stop Ares."

"What if you're wrong, Diana? What if there *is* no Ares?"

She gaped at him. "You don't believe me," she said. After all he had seen, all she had done, he still did not believe? No, he did not. He had lied to her, led her on all this time. Why? *To get off our island. To escape back into this blood-drenched world and its horrible war.* No matter. He had served as her messenger, summoning her to her destiny. Ares was real, and he was here.

But still, it hurt. Despite all appearances to the contrary, she was alone in a strange world. Her mission was not Steve's, and never would be.

He searched her face. "I can't let you do this."

"What I do is not up to you," she said. He held her tightly, as if to dispute that fact. She pushed him away with the tips of her fingers, expending the slightest effort but sending him reeling off-balance. Ignoring Steve's wounded expression, she looked around for Ludendorff.

He was nowhere to be seen.

He's gone! Diana thought, and she broke into a run. Grasping what was happening, Steve followed on her heels. Together they dashed around party guests and military officers, then burst outside through an open door.

There!

Steve joined her as they ran down a long dark hallway, bursting out onto a stone bridge. Ludendorff was disappearing through a turret door on their right. They began to follow; then there was a whoosh; they gazed up to the top of the turret as a projectile launched into the sky. It looked like a shooting star, but it was traveling away from the earth, not towards it. Fire arrows? No. No arrow could leave a trail of flame like that in its wake.

Coming up beside her out of breath, Steve wheezed, "The gas."

They stood shoulder to shoulder, watching the path of the missile across the sky. Diana calculated the trajectory in flight—and realized to her horror what the target was:

"The village!" she cried. Their village, Veld, all the people they had saved—

They ran then, across the bridge and past scattered partygoers who had come to see the show. A few startled glances were shot their way: a German officer pursuing a beautiful woman? Too much champagne?

Among the trees, Steve lost her as she dashed ahead and mounted her horse. She took off at a full gallop, and he could only watch.

In a fury, she raced against death, and time itself. The missile arched high up, up into the sky.

And then it disappeared over the horizon with its payload of death.

16

Lounging with the other chauffeurs, the whooshing sound made Sammy drop his Gunga Din act and look up, muttering curses in five languages. He knew that sound as he knew his mother's voice—a rocket had just launched—and he knew, given who was hosting this gala, what was likely riding on the tip of the projectile that had been sent off. He took a moment to scan for Steve, but didn't see him. He was worried for his leader, more worried still for whomever would be on the receiving end of the rocket's journey.

Plan B on all their ops was to rendezvous at the meeting point—in this case, back in the forest. Sammy knew it was time to go.

In all the hubbub, it was easy for him to jump back in the limousine. No one pursued; eyes were on the sky as he sped like the Devil himself, constantly checking the rearview mirror, hoping Steve had gotten away too.

Across the bridge, the guards unconcerned; back through the trees, so eerily calm; into the forest.

Spotting Charlie and the Chief, he hopped out of

the car. Coming alongside the Chief, he stared up at the exhaust trail that hung like strands of gray cotton in the night sky. Where was Diana?

Charlie was training his scope on the commotion at the castle.

"What are they cheering for?" Sammy asked.

He glanced over at the Scot as Charlie shifted his aim point, swinging it across the front of the building. Charlie abruptly lowered the rifle, an astonished look on his face. When Sammy turned back, his jaw dropped as he saw a figure on horseback, racing through the forest at tremendous speed—in the direction opposite of where they stood. It was the Amazon.

"Diana!" Sammy cried.

Next Steve galloped up on a horse as well, pulling hard on the reins, making his horse skid to the stop. Horse and rider were both out of breath. Steve didn't dismount.

"Where did they fire?" the Chief asked him.

"The gas. It was Ludendorff," Steve replied, which actually—tragically—answered the Chief's question.

Gas had already been Sammy's first guess; now that was confirmed. As a party favor, the German general had deployed the most terrible, the most indiscriminate weapon ever created. His last attempt, Sammy guessed, to derail Germany's surrender.

Charlie peered through his scope, scanning the grounds. "I saw. He's on the tower," he announced.

"Where he goes, you follow him," Steve said. Then he wheeled his horse around, applied his spurs, and took off after Diana.

"How will you find us?" Sammy called after him.

"I know how," the Chief assured Sammy.

This stupid dress. It encumbered Diana, making it difficult for her to sit astride a horse that was running full tilt. She ripped it off and flung it into the air. The fabric floated down on the path behind her like a trail of blue smoke. Leaning over the horse's neck as it raced, she spoke into its ear. "Faster," she urged. "Faster."

The horse reared its head, eyes wild, and then laid its ears back and valiantly put on a burst of speed. The trees blurred, the impacts of the horse's hooves rippled through Diana's legs and up her backbone. She drove her mount to its breaking point, and held it there. Lives hung in the balance.

Then she heard and felt the explosion. Very close. Close enough to make the ground shake and the horse falter in mid-stride and catch itself. She pressed her knees to its flanks, urging it forward. She would not stop until she had done whatever she could for Veld.

Seconds later, when they burst out of the forest, the field in front of them was draped in noxious, swirling fog. She should have been able to see the village from here, but she could not. Everything was blanketed in bright orange poison gas.

Diana pulled back on the reins; no need for this faithful horse to be harmed. She dismounted. It whickered; she patted it to stay and then she ran forward into the acrid orange smoke.

Into the valley of death.

The square loomed before her, barely visible in the clouds of gas.

The pretty little café with its awnings.

Gone. Blasted to bits.

The tables grouped around the fountain.

Gone.

The inn.

Gone.

But the victims were not gone. They lay where they had collapsed, almost as if they were asleep. People she had danced with, shared bread with. The woman who had pleaded with her to save them. The people who had shaken her hands. The photographer. All dead.

"No. Oh no, no, no," she whispered, raking her hands through her hair, pressing her hands against her temples, as she staggered through the fog. The uncanny, unnatural stillness. Silence. This place, a tomb.

I failed them. I knew he was Ares and I did not act.

The poison still lingered over the square, as if seeking one last victim. She wandered in a daze, unable to comprehend the souls of men who could create such evil. To deliberately wipe out an entire village like this. To do it from afar, in their safe castle with their champagne and waltzes. Without honor, preying on the innocent. They could only have been inspired by Ares, mass-murderer of the Gods and of this world.

Then she saw the little children she had seen chasing each other through the square. Their parents, this world, robbed of them. Their lives stolen. The human sacrifices *he* had boasted of. And for what?

For what?

This was her breaking point. This was her final call to action. Nothing would stop her, nothing. Collision course. Fate. Destiny. Though it cost her everything:

Ares, I am coming for you now.

I will not let you see another sunset.

* * *

Veld.

Steve leaped off his horse and raced toward the bright orange cloud, aware of the death it carried and that Diana was probably already in there. But as he reached the edge of the poison fog he began to hack and cough. Still he stumbled forward.

Then a dark form took shape in the middle of the cloud, growing more and more distinct as it moved towards him. His heart pounded; he trembled with hope. *Let it be her. By some miracle, let her be all right.*

Diana stepped from the smoke, completely unhurt.

"Diana! Diana!" he shouted, his heart soaring.

He swung down from the saddle and ran across the field to her. She raised her arm and pointed at him. "They're dead. They're all dead!" Her voice shook with barely controlled rage. Her eyes flashed with anger. "I could have saved them. I could have saved them if it weren't for *you*!"

Rattled, he held out his hands to her. She kept her distance. "You stopped me from killing Ares!"

He reached for her. "No."

"*Stay away from me!*" she shouted. "Now I understand everything. It isn't just the Germans he's corrupted. It is you too. All of you."

He knew she was in shock, in terrible pain. Had seen hell first hand. Behind her, the cloud of gas began to lift and disperse, its terrible damage already done. They were too late, and he had known they would be too late. He had told her about this war—the scope of it, the savagery. But he could not have hoped to prepare her for it. What was happening—had happened—was unthinkable. And he was sorry, so very sorry, that he couldn't make it vanish with a sword thrust.

She looked hard into his eyes and said, "I will find Ares and I will kill him."

What could he say? How could he argue? Before he could respond, a trail of smoke in the sky caught his attention. Not the arc of another missile. This plume drifted straight up. A smoke signal, created in the Native American fashion, to announce to Steve that the team had picked up Ludendorff's trail.

"Diana," he said, "that smoke. It's the Chief. They followed Ludendorff. Follow the smoke."

Before he could say another word, she leaped onto the back of her horse and rode off like a whirlwind.

"Diana!" he called after her. He had meant that they should follow it together. He started to get back onto his own horse; then as the poison cloud continued to dissipate, he spotted an abandoned motorcycle on the side of the road that led into the village. He ran over to it, pulled it upright, and straddled the seat. He put his right foot on the starter pedal, bracing his left foot on the ground.

Let it start, he prayed as he stomped the pedal. The engine caught on the first try, roaring to life with a twist of the throttle.

Someone, somewhere was listening.

I will run him to ground.

Diana flew through the dark forest, giving her horse its head, trusting it to know the true path. The reins dangled loose in her hands as she gripped the horse's mane and pressed her things against its flanks, making horse and rider one. The stalwart animal dodged tree trunks and veered around low-hanging branches, vaulting ditches with the heart and skill of a warhorse. They burst out onto the main road and the horse's iron-shod hooves sparked as they crashed down.

If the team had Ludendorff in sight, there was still a chance to destroy him. She couldn't take Ares by surprise as she had planned, but take him she would. Face to face, toe to toe. To the death. This would be his last night on Earth, the end of his reign over mankind. Veld would be his final abomination.

Over the horse's bobbing head, she saw that the way was blocked by a security checkpoint. The Germans had set up a barrier to traffic, or what they thought would be a barrier. As she galloped toward it, two of the soldiers stepped out in front and one of them raised a gloved hand for her to stop. When she didn't slow down, the guards exchanged worried looks, then in unison shouldered their rifles. Before they could fire, she was on them. She split the space between them and her horse's wide shoulders, knocked them aside like bowling pins a second before it launched itself over the barrier. The third sentry backed out of the way. He was too stunned to raise his weapon.

Diana gave the horse a nudge with her spurs, rounding a bend in the road, putting herself well out of range.

Steve had the motorcycle throttle wide open, trying to get within sight of Diana. But he couldn't seem to catch up to her no matter how fast he went. Soon he became unsure whether she was still ahead of him at all. Perhaps she had veered off the path? But where? He slowed down a bit, hoping to pick up her trail. He quickly gave that up as pointless and killed the engine. He strained to hear the beat of horse hooves, but the only sound was the soft wind in the treetops.

He restarted the engine and drove on. Down the road a quarter mile, he spotted a security post. Confident his German uniform would protect him from a potshot, he rode closer—close enough to see the soldiers manning the barrier looked injured and dazed. One of them was clutching his arm like it was broken. No doubt about it, Diana had passed this way. He felt a surge of relief that he was on the right track and gunned the engine to pick up speed. Then he turned the bike into the forest, roaring off through the trees.

Diana looked up as she rode on, searching for the sign in the sky. Patches of deepening darkness were already cloaking the canopied trail. Her anxiety building, she pressed on through the forest, urging her mount to speed up its headlong gallop.

She smelled the wood smoke long before she saw it rising up through a gap in the branches. Finally, a course to follow. She spurred the horse, turning it toward the thin gray column. Then she caught a flicker of orange flame through the trees. Charlie, the Chief, and Sammy stood around the fire they had made.

Spotting her before the others, the Chief raised his hand and pointed to the top of the hill beyond them.

Charlie and Sammy looked at her expectantly. From their body language, Diana realized they thought she was going to dismount and confer with them before proceeding. There was no chance of that, not if Ares was near.

Her horse flicked its tail as she cantered into the clearing toward the three men. When they realized she wasn't going to stop, their faces fell, and they hurriedly stepped aside.

Her path clear, she dug in her spurs, and the horse took off up the grade.

Steve's heart leapt when he finally got a glimpse of a horse and rider racing ahead. Then they vanished around a bend. He twisted the throttle wide open, trying to close the distance. Skidding around a turn carpeted with damp leaves and pine needles, he put his foot down to keep the bike upright, then roared onto a straightaway. Then he spotted her.

It's Diana!

As he continued to accelerate, Steve saw her gallop past the others without stopping. When she turned to race up the hill, he lost sight of her again. But not for long. Redlining the engine, bending over the handlebars to reduce wind resistance, he whipped by Charlie, Sammy, and the Chief at seventy miles an hour, pelting them with sticks and dirt. Then he slowed to make the turn up the hill after her.

The team raced up the incline after him.

17

From the summit, Diana gazed down on a cluster of buildings bordered by a long, flat area on which aeroplanes sat parked. It was a German airfield, like the one Steve had described during his interrogation on Themyscira, encircled by two high, barbed-wire fences—perhaps erected to keep their slave labor contained. She heard a dull whirring sound and looked more closely. Two of the flying machines had their engines idling. She could see the propellers spinning. The site was crawling with German soldiers. They marched back and forth, working on the planes, entering and leaving buildings, moving heavy carts loaded with wooden crates.

It occurred to her that Ares didn't need a German aeroplane to make his escape; a God had the power to fly on his own, without mechanical or any other kind of assistance. But if Ares wanted to remain in his human disguise, he could easily put an insurmountable distance between himself and pursuit, simply by climbing into one of the machines and taking it where he wanted to go. That idea sent a fresh wave of urgency flooding through her.

She could not lose him now. She could not let that happen.

Carefully she scanned the field, the planes, the nest of low buildings, and the tall structure that towered over them. She saw soldiers in twos and threes—no entourages—yet Ludendorff was not the kind of man to travel without one. Her vantage point was too distant and the angle of sight too steep; half the compound was hidden from view. To find him she had to get nearer. Much nearer.

Spurring her horse, she stormed down the hillside, keeping to the tree line as much as possible. Dark horse, dark rider, dark forest. With any luck the Germans wouldn't see her until it was too late.

As she descended, she kept her eyes on the compound, trusting the horse to find its own footing. Something moved near the top of the tall structure, which was, on closer inspection, a wooden tower line with metal stairs. There was a platform on the upper story, a railed balcony, and guard standing outside.

She felt a sudden catch in her throat, then a rush of excitement. Ludendorff was inside the tower!

At the base of the slope, she turned the horse toward the barbed wire and charged. On the other side of the fence a small clutch of German soldiers saw her movements and reacted, raising weapons.

This was as close to the tower as she could get, and she had to act quickly before they sounded the alarm. Without a second's hesitation, she leaped off her horse and twirled over the top of the fence, landing just behind a second fence. She rushed forward, swinging the Godkiller overhead. No jumping this time. Slashing the blade back and forth she hacked through the coils of wire like a stand of thorny dry weeds.

The cluster of Germans went on the offensive, rushing her. There was no time for the niceties. Diana ducked under an out-thrust rifle. Effortlessly, she turned and grabbed the man with the rifle by the hips and spun him around 360 degrees. Then she toppled each one in turn, racing to silence them before they raised the cry.

It was over in seconds.

Beyond them, across the open field on which the planes were parked, loomed the tower. It was constructed of wood crisscrossing metal beams, and the stairs went all the way up to the roof.

Diana saw a straight track to her goal, and she took it. At the base of the tower, she buckled her shield to her back. Unlimbering the Lasso of Hestia, she swung its loop around and around over her head, building momentum; then she let it fly straight up. The slack rope slithered up behind it, peeling from her open hand. The glowing loop dropped neatly over the soldier's helmet, past his nose, and under his chin. He jerked back in surprise, which only tightened the loop. As he leaned forward to relieve the pressure, Diana pulled down hard. The soldier flipped over the railing and fell, flailing all the way to the ground. She used the momentum to propel herself up to the balcony. She landed, scanning her surroundings. The ladder was the only way up and down from the top—not counting the deadfall. Unless Ares shed his human form and showed the world what he really was, she had him trapped.

If Ares had decided to meet her halfway, it might have been difficult—but he didn't. He was nowhere in sight as she darted across the balcony floor. Panes of glass encircled the interior, which was the control room of the flight tower. Seated at a desk, a young German soldier wearing a headset was oblivious of her presence. She entered the room with the Godkiller in her hand, tore the headset off of him, and tossed him off the balcony.

And there he was—Ludendorff. Alone. With his steel-gray and his imposing size, a precise German officer.

A God in disguise.

Ludendorff turned as she approached him. He looked her up and down, lingering on the sword she held; then his mouth twisted into a smirk.

"What a surprise," he said. He cocked his head as he took in her appearance—an Amazon in battle gear. "Strange." With icy efficiency, he plucked a small gun from his jacket pocket and pointed it at her. "Unfortunately, I have another matter to attend to."

With that, he fired. The pistol bucked in his hand and the first bullet left the barrel. It was faster than sound, but so was Diana. She blocked it with her bracelet, and in the same instant that the sharp report rocked the little room, the bullet reversed course, ricocheting back down the barrel just as Ludendorff fired a second shot. It was the first time she had directed a bullet with her bracelets, and she realized that she had just provided herself with another weapon.

The gun barrel exploded in his hand. He shrieked in pain, letting the weapon drop to the floor. His face twisted in a grimace as he clutched his fingers.

It was an excellent performance, but he wasn't fooling her. He was a God and he would heal just as quickly as she had at the site of his most recent atrocity. Whatever advantage she had gained against him would evaporate in an instant.

"What are you?" he demanded.

"You will soon find out." She spun the Godkiller in her grip, preparing for battle. She was an Amazon. She was a defender, protector. And she was here to save the world.

He turned away, reaching into his pocket, taking something out, then hunching over. She was prepared to fend off a new weapon, a different attack, but none appeared. There was an audible snap, like a dry stick breaking. She heard him inhale deeply; then he let out a groan and shuddered. There was a strange odor that she hadn't noticed before; she couldn't remember smelling anything quite like it. The closest thing that came to mind was the fumes from the traffic in London. When he turned back toward her, he had changed, and the transformation was startling. The veins on his face, neck, and hands were bulging hideously, like knotted ropes under his skin. His face was *glowing*.

Ares the God was also a monster: a monster she had come to kill.

She attacked, thrusting the Godkiller at him with all the force she could muster just as he reached over and ripped a bulky metal warming stove from the wall. With ease he flung it at her; it broke apart against her, the metal clattering against the walls and floor.

Taking advantage of her surprise, he sprang on her, grabbed her up, and threw her against a window. It shattered around her, glass flying everywhere, catching light as it cascaded and fell. Then he shoved a table into her midsection, pinning her—but only momentarily. She pushed it out of the way and came at him, smashing him in the face with her fist. His head barely moved.

Circling in the cramped space, they traded

barehanded blows. Each of them shifted just enough, blocked just enough to spoil the effect of the punches. Then he caught her with a straight right hand to the chin that sent her skidding backwards.

Diana feinted right, and as he swung on her, she ducked under the blow and, pivoting from the balls of her feet, slammed the pommel of the Godkiller into the side of his head. He jerked hard. The Godkiller made the difference.

As he recovered his feet and turned, he glared at her, then darted his glance around the room. A rifle with bayonet was hanging on hooks on the wall. He snatched it free and swung it around, slashing it back and forth like a sword. She used the Godkiller to fend off the attack, knocked the bayonet blade aside, and snap kicked him in the stomach.

He turned the rifle butt-end and slammed it against her over and over. She had easily withstood the force of a rifle smashed across her back, but the pressure of his blows made her knees buckle. Ares was getting stronger rather than weaker. She fell to the floor, dropping the Godkiller. Before she could recover, he scooped it up.

"As magnificent as you are, you are still no match for me," he crowed.

"We'll see about that," she countered.

The veins in his face looked as if they were about to burst. He was working himself up to make a final attack. He brought down the blade; still prone, she caught it between her palms and grabbed it away from him. The raw blade in her hand filled her with strength and courage. She had sworn to free mankind from Ares's thrall. And with this precious gift, she would do it.

The look of surprise on his face energized her. She

bent her legs and sprung up, smashing him in the stomach, putting every ounce of power into the punch. He flew backwards and crashed through one of the windows, landing on his back on the narrow walkway that ran around the tower.

As he struggled to his feet, Diana jumped through the empty window frame after him. She slashed down with the Godkiller, but her quarry rolled away. He came up with his back to the railing. She had him. She aimed the sword thrust to split his heart, and it would have if he hadn't twisted away at the last second. The blade's edge made a shrill screech as it scraped across the steel.

He jumped onto the rail and from there scrambled on the ladder to the tower's roof.

She blasted through the ceiling, soaring high above the tower into the sky, the very heavens themselves. She looked down. Ludendorff/Ares had remained below on the roof, poised to take her on. She landed and faced him. Faced him down, the evil God who had brought such misery to the villagers in Veld. Through history, to millions. Before history: the God who had killed all the other Gods.

The God who could be killed only by an Amazon with the Godkiller in her grip. She pulled free the Lasso of Hestia.

"I am Diana of Themyscira. Daughter of Hippolyta, Queen of the Amazons. And your wrath upon this world is over," she said, offering honor in her declaration despite his craven lack of it.

She lassoed Ludendorff. Throwing him high into the air, she flew upward with the momentum. They both soared with the night wind, the lasso gleaming against the smoke. Twisting, spiral, she kept hold of him. She had made a vow in Themyscira. She had renewed that vow in Veld. And she was a woman of her word.

She landed back down first. Pulling the lasso sharply, she smacked him onto the roof. He came down hard on his back. A mortal man would be dead by now.

He looked up at her. She stood over him, holding the Godkiller above her head. Her chest heaved. Was there fear in his eyes? Did he know that he was going to die?

"In the name of all that is good in this world, I hereby complete the mission of the Amazons, ridding this world of you forever."

He began to raise up. With a mighty downward thrust, she stabbed him in the chest. He fell back against the tower roof. His distorted veins faded. His eyes remained open, sightless. She had done it. She had dispatched Ares, traitor to gods, betrayer of humanity, enemy of all that was good. Diana stared down at him.

She had killed him.

Ares, God of War, was dead by her hand.

Let it be so, then.

In the next split-second, a frenzy of lightning strobed and exploded, enveloping the control tower.

Flashing, sizzling, shooting everywhere.

Blue-white energy; a whirlwind, a vortex.

The volcanic explosion billowed outward, a brilliant mushroom cloud of blinding light. Atomic, a comet firing. The sky shook. Along her arms, her bracelets sizzled. Diana stood in the center of it with the inert body of Ares at her feet. The discharge of his life force? The restoration of the balance of the universe—the power of rightness that he had stolen from mankind? She did not know. Energy raged around her, uncontrollable; and then, all at once, it dissipated.

The entire structure plunged into darkness. Stillness. Exhaustion, relief beyond the telling, Diana raised her face toward the sky. It was over. Now mankind would return to a world filled with kindness and bliss. It would be a paradise like she had known on Themyscira.

It would be what it had been meant to be.

The serenity.

The calm before.

Before the storm

On the tower roof, Diana opened her eyes as thunder rumbled in the distance. Above her, clouds in the ebony sky billowed and puffed upwards, blocking out the stars. It was a storm, simmering—perhaps about to bring a cleansing rain to refresh the wounded earth. Leaching out the poison, watering seeds and roots to grow living things again.

Suddenly a voice from below the tower started shouting in German: *"Schnell! Geh' geh'!"* Quickly! Go, go!

Diana looked from the sky to the airfield below, and her breath caught in her throat.

Soldiers in strange masks poured out of the buildings, pushing carts filled with what looked like metal pineapples. She knew from the photographs in the London war room and Steve's own descriptions that these were the infamous gas bombs of Dr. Maru. It had taken only one to destroy the town of Veld. Here there were hundreds.

Aeroplane propellers still whirred. The soldiers still moved the bombs filled with Dr. Maru's poison along the tracks in the ground. They had been preparing to take the war somewhere else. To do to other villages what they had done to Veld, but now they would stop.

Now.

Except they didn't. They continued as if nothing had happened. As if Ares had not died. She glanced back down at him. He was most surely dead.

She stood frozen. Horror gripped her hard as she tried to make sense of it. They should have stopped. Nothing had changed. The war continued. But Ares was *dead*.

The masked, hooded soldiers fanned out like anonymous insects, cogs in the machinery of death.

But I freed them from his tyranny.

Yet the soldiers continued on their way, rushing, hurrying to fulfill the order to kill their fellow man.

"Diana!" Steve called. He saw her silhouetted on the roof. She was still alive, despite the massive explosion that he had assumed had leveled the tower. He had no idea what had happened and at the moment he didn't care; on legs made rubbery with relief, he climbed to the balcony of the control tower.

From this vantage point, he could see the airfield and the hangar. Smoke was streaming from one of the smokestacks. Maru's lab? He looked at the German soldiers in their masks as they wheeled cart after cart of gas bombs out of the hanger. Dear God, they were preparing to transport the gas somewhere else—stockpiling it for another poison gas attack, Armistice or no. His espionage-trained mind ran through various schemes to stop it—all starring the Amazonian princess on the roof above him.

But Diana's eyes were wide and vacant. He knew that look; it was shellshock. He had seen it before, many times. In the trenches and the war rooms, on the faces of doughboys and generals. She simply could not process what was happening around her—the plans for murder on a vast scale unfolding around them.

Then he spotted a body unmoving at Diana's feet. He looked more closely; it was General Ludendorff. To all appearances dead, her sword plunged into his chest. So she had done it—killed the German she believed to be the root cause of all this war's crimes against humanity. The bad guy. She had fulfilled her mission. How, then, to explain the utter disbelief on her face?

"I killed him," she declared. "I killed him but nothing stopped." She blinked, bewildered. "You kill the God of War, you stop the war."

He nodded vigorously, glad to have her back. "Exactly what we have to do now." He spoke urgently. They had so little time to do what they had come here to do. Stop this. Stop all of this.

She jumped down from the roof and landed next to him. She looked unsteady. Exhausted, he assumed. Even an Amazon must get tired.

"We need to stop the gas," he said. "Come on."

He turned to go. But it was clear that she wasn't with him. Distracted, lost, she looked down at the activity in a daze, as if she couldn't believe her eyes.

"No. All this should have stopped."

"Diana," he pressed. They could sort that out later.

After surviving everything they had endured to locate the manufacturing site, they couldn't hesitate now. This was the mission they had agreed on—to do what they could to stop the war. They stood not just in the belly of the beast, but in its heart and soul. There would be other battles other days, but without this hellish weapon, Germany would submit to peace.

"The fighting should have stopped." Her voice cracked.

His heart trip hammered against his ribs. God, *God*; his nerves sizzled like live wires. Every second they stood here was another chance that the mission would fail. They could not fail.

"We don't have time to talk about this." He wanted to shout at her but he kept his voice steady. Not now. Now now. They were so close. Too close.

Below him, the German troops kept rolling the carts out of the warehouse. Time was ticking past. They had a window of opportunity that would eventually slam shut. Charlie, Sammy, and the Chief were waiting for instructions. Down there they were sitting ducks. He had to get to them with a plan *now*.

Her eyes were enormous, her face pale. "*Why are they doing this?*"

"I don't know." That was honest. There was no answer for that question, and he had long ago stopped asking it. He didn't have that luxury. And neither did she. Not then.

"Ares is dead. They can stop fighting now. Why are they still fighting?" she asked brokenly.

And then he realized how hard a moment this was for her. A bitter, bitter pill. The culmination of her entire mission—she had left *everything* behind, risked her life over and over again—and from her view, all of it had been for nothing. Her entire identity had rested on stopping this war by killing Ares. And it had not worked. He understood how that felt. That terrible, crushing sense of disillusionment. He tuned in to her, made himself present for her, finding his way to her despite the terrible pressure of their situation.

"Maybe because it's them. Maybe people are not always good. Ares or no Ares. Maybe it's who they are." He looked hard at her, aware that in his passion he was almost yelling. Saving humanity was their shared passion. That was why she had gone after Ares. The end goal was still the same. "Diana, please. I need you come with me."

She stiffened; then she shook her head. "No."

He was stunned. She meant it. He couldn't let her do this. He needed her. The world needed her. "Diana, please."

"No," she said again. "After everything I saw, it can't be. It cannot be." She looked at him but he could tell that she wasn't seeing him. She was seeing the tragedy of Veld. The horribly maimed soldiers staggering off the hospital ship. The shattered men in the trenches of No Man's Land. Orphans. Widows. She could not have imagined such horrors growing up on Themyscira.

"They were killing each other," she said. "Killing people they cannot see. Children. *Children. No.*" Her expression clouded; her expression pleaded for this to make sense. "It had to be him. It cannot be them."

"Diana…" He struggled to find the words to snap her out of this. Not, not just that. To make their partnership whole again. To work side by side again. To be together again.

To be together.

"My mother was right. She said 'the world of men doesn't deserve you. She was right." She shook her head. "They don't deserve our help."

"It's not about deserve," Steve declared, then added, more gently, "Maybe we don't, but it's not about that. It's about what you believe." When she parted her lips to protest, he continued. "You don't think I get it? All I've seen out here? You don't think I wish I could tell you that it was one bad guy to blame? We're all to blame." *And we need your help. I need your help. Diana—*

She flared. "I'm not."

"But maybe I am." Urgency pumped through his veins. After everything they had gone through to get here, this could not be where and how it ended. He needed her help. Desperately. "Please, if you believe this war should stop, if you want to stop it, then help me stop it right now. Because if you don't, they will kill thousands more." She had to know that. Had to believe that. It was the truth, as horrible as it was. It hinged on her.

She remained silent.

"Please, come with me. I have to go. I have to go." Any second now, they would be taken prisoner, if not shot on sight. Was the team watching and waiting for his signal? Wondering what the holdup was? *Come on, Diana. Come on, come on. Please.*

That she was still in crisis was written all over her face. She hadn't made the connection that to him seemed so obvious. Ludendorff was just a man who had chosen an evil path. That gave him no special power except the authority granted to him by other men. For everything he had done, every act of cruelty, he had been granted license to do so by other men. That meant he had not acted alone.

But that also meant he could be stopped by men.

By them.

That was easy for Steve to grasp because he had lived all his life in this cold, cruel reality. In this world, you couldn't blame a malevolent deity for the sins of human beings.

But in Diana's world, you could blame a God, and your people did, for thousands of years. Diana's mother had told her the story of Ares since she was a little girl. That idea had bored deep into Diana's heart—into her very soul. It had given her life meaning, purpose. To excuse the entire human race for warring on each other because they were subject to the whims of a God, and to free them from the yoke of oppression by taking him on in battle.

The grace she had offered mankind was misplaced.

He didn't want to say any of that to her. But he needed her to get past her moment of doubt so they could stop the enemy who was right under their noses. Given half a chance, Maru would inflict as much suffering as she possibly could with Germany's new secret weapon until whole nations bowed down to the Kaiser. Steve knew that as surely as he knew his own name. And he had to do something about it. If he could have spared Diana this horrible revelation, he would have. But he needed her too much.

Shaking her head in denial, she looked at the swarms of soldiers bent on destruction and killing—moving of their own free will, not under the thrall of Ares.

"No," she said. She was turning him down. Refusing to go on. She had had her fill.

He was staggered.

And he left her there.
He left her.
He left.

Steve returned empty-handed to Charlie, Sammy, and the Chief, who were waiting for him around the corner of a building next to the airstrip. The trio was crouched in a defensive posture, facing in different directions—ready to return fire no matter where it came from. He didn't ask them how they'd managed to cross the heavily guarded compound without raising an alarm. Charlie and the Chief lowered their weapons, and looked at him hopefully.

Sammy frowned and looked past him. "Where's Diana?" he asked.

"We're on our own," Steve said curtly, and didn't elaborate. He turned to the Scot. "What do you see, Charlie?"

"It looks like a bunch of gas bombs. But I can't see where they're taking them." That dovetailed with Steve's own observations.

"How're we gonna get in there?" the Chief asked.

Kind of ironic, him asking that. *The way in is through the gate.* It always had been, in essence, a rhetorical question. Steve's team had rarely failed to infiltrate any field of engagement they had set their minds to. But this was no time for pipes and turbans. The field was crawling with Germans soldiers, and this was no gala. This was the very serious business of war.

Steve took in their surroundings, scouting for potential shields and possible weapons. Then he signaled for his squad to form up and advance on his order.

He waited for a breach in the lines of the onrushing

enemy, saw it, and gave the signal. He knew without looking that Charlie, Sammy, and the Chief immediately fell into line behind him. He was grateful down to the soles of his boots that they had stuck around for this. Heroes, each one. If only Diana—

No time for that now.

They were on the move, Steve seeking their next vantage point, where they could see what was going on without revealing themselves. A hard nut to crack under the circumstances. It would require only one sharp-eyed soldier to sound the alarm.

A couple of things were working in their favor, though: an air of frenzy in the compound, as if everyone was rushing to meet some critical deadline. Another positive: the soldiers were wearing gas hoods, which limited their field of vision.

Steve took a deep breath as they gained ground. When they halted, he slowly let it out. It was time to puzzle out a strategy and get 'er done.

Then Sammy gestured to some German soldiers lying unconscious—Diana's doing, Steve guessed, before she checked out.

"I've got an idea," Sammy said. "Come on, guys."

They ran in concert toward the fallen soldiers.

BOOK III
WONDER WOMAN

"The secret to happiness is freedom... and the secret to freedom is courage."
—Thucydides

18

The world of men was hell. And they had built it themselves.

Diana looked down from the balcony of the control tower at organized chaos. The soldiers scrambling around were like insect drones serving their monstrous queen. Pandora's box had been opened, and men, not evils, had bounded out. Men were the evils. This was the chapter Diana would add to the story of her people if she were ever so fortunate as to see her homeland again.

Her fists were balled. Her mind reeled. For what seemed like a very long time, she felt nothing. But slowly, inexorably, the world outside penetrated her numbness. The chill wind from the storm. The even colder drops of rain. The crash of thunder coming closer. Then the stink of chemicals and the insanity of mechanical noise. She had traded away paradise, and for what?

She had been such a fool. Not a hero on a quest, but a deluded, hapless wanderer. How certain she had been of her truth, the truth of the Amazons—that they had been created to bring peace to this world by destroying Ares, who held humanity in thrall. That was their story, the only story she had ever known. Her thoughts arranged and rearranged themselves in her mind. *Have I gone crazy? Did I misunderstand? Was my mother's story only a lullaby to calm a restless little girl to sleep? But then why the training? And the hiding? Our home was concealed, our powers cloaked from the eyes of the world for a reason.*

Why else, but to defend ourselves from these… goblins if ever should they find their way onto our shores. And they did. And they cut the greatest of us down without hesitation.

Steve was the first.

Steve Trevor. The first man to touch the sands of her home. The first man who had touched her. She had to believe that he was good. Or else she was the greatest fool in this horrible realm.

She reminded herself of Veld. He had risked his life to save the villagers. He had asked, begged, pleaded for her to help him save more people like them. And she had let him go.

My foreordinance. What do I really believe?

She blinked, hearing someone inside the control tower. She turned. Through the balcony windows she could see a male figure, his back turned to her. For a moment she thought that Steve had returned one last time to ask her to do her duty. This time she would say—

—She would say…

That was not Steve. He was too short. And he wasn't wearing a German uniform. As if sensing her presence, the man stiffened but didn't turn around. She remained on the balcony, on her guard.

"Who's there?" she demanded.

Keeping his back to her, the man said in English,

"I've been waiting for you to see the truth."

That voice. Not German, nor American—he had a British accent. And it was a voice she recognized. But it didn't make sense that he would be here, and out in the open like this.

"Sir Patrick?" she said, wary, confused.

Slowly turning, Sir Patrick calmly gazed at her through the pane of glass. Something was not right. Had something happened? Why was he so calm?

She stared at the kindly gentleman who had worked so hard to help Steve, his men, and her get to this heavily fortified German stronghold, but who should be back in England with Etta Candy. They had spoken on the phone only yesterday, and they hadn't checked in since. He had forbidden them to undertake this mission. And yet he seemed unsurprised to see her.

She tried to understand why he wasn't undercover himself. Why he was smiling while he stood in the heart of this German weapons facility.

And suddenly, inexplicably she *knew*. Every sense fired as she the truth crashed down on her.

Ludendorff was not Ares. Sir Patrick was.

This seemingly frail, aged man was her sworn enemy, and the enemy of all her people. The duplicitous warmonger who reveled in death and destruction.

No. This made no sense. She was wrong. He was just a man. And a man of peace at that. In the War Council, he had argued that the Armistice must be made. While they were in Veld, he had forbidden Diana, Steve, and the team to interfere in any way before that Armistice was signed.

And then he made sure to send us to the Front. And to

tell us about the gala knowing full well that we wouldn't listen to him when he told us not to go. That we would do everything in our power to find and infiltrate this base.

He manipulated our every move because he knew that we would do what good people do. We would risk everything to protect the world. Except that I—

I lost heart. But this is my chance. This is my foreordinance. He is Ares, and I must destroy him. It begins here. The story of my fate.

"You're right, Diana," he said with an unctuous smile. "They don't deserve our help."

His smile widened at her surprise as he tossed her own words—her mother's words—back at her: Either he had been hiding in the shadows, standing close enough to listen in on the conversation she'd just had with Steve—her disdain of humanity—or he had powers of hearing beyond imagining. More proof, then, that he was the God she sought. And that she had a chance to redeem herself. Here. Now. If she was right. She had been wrong once, and killed a man—admittedly a very evil man—in fulfillment of her mission.

Eyes glittering, Sir Patrick paused as if to savor the moment. As if he had been anticipating it for millennia.

He rendered his final verdict: "They only deserve destruction."

"You. You're *him*," she affirmed.

"I am," he said, raising his chin and taking on the rightful bearing of a son of Zeus. He was brother to the exalted pantheon of Olympians he had slain. "But I'm not what you thought I was." With a sweep of his arm he motioned at the airfield, the planes, the armed men scurrying in gas masks. "You blame me, but the truth is… all of this… I did none of it."

Liar, she thought. *You are the father of lies, and of betrayal.*

She reached for the Godkiller—but she had left it on the roof, with Ludendorff. As she whirled around and headed for the roof, his smile followed her like a fist of black cloud.

Charlie, Steve, Sammy, and the Chief hunkered down inside the open doorway of one of the field's outbuildings. Frustrated, they observed the seemingly endless parade of masked soldiers moving crate after crate of gas bombs out of the hanger, but they had yet to find Dr. Maru's lab or Dr. Maru herself. If they didn't get her notes and, preferably, her, she would take everything with her that she needed to resume manufacture of her lethal gas bombs in another lab.

Charlie raised his rifle to his shoulder and peered through the scope. After diligently scanning the area, he shook his head and said, "I can't see where they're taking the gas."

Steve slipped out of the doorway and waved for everyone to follow. Charlie kept his Lee–Enfield ready, lowered his head, and brought up the rear. Steve was moving them closer to the hangar itself. It wouldn't be the first time they had fought in close quarters, but he still preferred long-distance targets. Ironically, while this lot was faceless, he'd have felt a lot better if they weren't wearing masks. Their ghostly appearance took him back to Edinburgh and nights by the fireside listening to tales of ghosties and ghoulies.

More gas-masked soldiers appeared from around the next corner, marching directly in front of them. Moving as one, the team took cover behind a stack of wooden crates. The pounding of the Germans' feet vibrated through the ground. So many, stamping about like bizarre clockwork figures in their masks, the faceless enemy. Where would it all end?

From his vantage point, Sammy took in the grim hustle of the rank and file and wondered at the need for urgency. There was a reason the Germans were trying to get the gas out of here so fast. Did they plan to lock it away before the Armistice was signed? Use it for revenge or to weaken the Allies as much as possible before they were forced to lay down arms as part of the peace process? Sell it to the highest bidder? No good could come of it, no matter what they did with it.

Motion in his peripheral vision startled him.

Oh, no. No.

His lips parted in a silent shout as he raised his hand to point across the airfield.

Suddenly it all made terrible sense.

And from the looks on the others' faces, they were just as stunned as he was.

Charlie looked to where Sammy had indicated and muttered a multisyllabic curse in Gaelic. *What the hell?*

"What is it?" the Chief asked.

"The future," Steve replied grimly.

An aircraft as huge as the Loch Ness Monster was being towed along the airstrip by a chugging truck. Never in his life had he seen a flying machine so gigantic.

He'd never even dreamed you could build a monster like that. A black biplane, it was easily seventy-five feet long. It was mounted with four huge engines, and the blades were whirring. The Germans were actually going to fly it. Unless the good guys had a few tricks up their sleeve, their side was outgunned. *We need a mad scientist or two of our own.*

Then he saw that the door in the side of the fuselage was open, and he put two and two together. He didn't like the result. The masked soldiers and workers in coveralls were taking the weapons from their crates and very carefully passing them to crewmen crouched inside the plane. They were going to fill that behemoth with ugly death and it was going to lift off with an unbelievable arsenal of mass destruction in its belly. A plane that size could carry a hundred bombs. Maybe more. And it could still fly? The aerodynamics of such a beast were beyond his ken, but this much he knew: he was staring at a doomsday machine.

Charlie peered through his scope. The crewmen were loading the bomb bay under the supervision of an officer who was likely the commander or the pilot. There were a lot of men in the crew, six or seven by his count.

A sharp gust of black wind swept over the field. It was so cold it made Charlie cringe. A dust cloud raced across the field, and the dual wings of the monstrous bomber shivered. Overhead, the sky was roiling in shades of black and gray. Altogether an inauspicious set of circumstances. Would it delay takeoff?

A soldier near the plane's tail used his bayonet to gesture impatiently at workers loading more bombs through a smaller door. The weapons were being stored back in the aft, Charlie realized. The bomb bay doors had to be located there, then. The bomber had surplus explosives on hand beyond any bombing run he could imagine. Under no circumstances could the team allow it to fly away. If even a fraction of that payload was dropped on a defenseless city, the death toll would be in the hundreds of thousands, if not millions. With four engines to power it, the bomber had to have a range of close to five hundred miles. Enough range to strike multiple cities across Europe and Britain.

The Chief shifted beside his teammates. At the sight of the huge black bomber, the tension among them had ratcheted up. This was no simple smuggling operation to get the gas bombs out of the Allies' reach in the event of an armistice. The team's objective had just spit into two: One, they had to get Dr. Maru and her formula; and two, they had to stop this bomber from ever taking off.

This was an altogether different game plan for a smuggler. But like so much of life, what mattered was what you did when confronted with the unexpected. And he would do what was right—no matter the cost. So much for coming to this war for profit.

The four men watched in horror for a few more seconds; then Steve gestured for them to pull back, and they headed around the back of the hanger.

Whatever I do, I must hold myself together, Charlie told himself. *My hands must not shake. My aim must be true.*

It had meant a lot that Steve had sought him out, still believed in him. He was determined to do all he could to keep and build that trust. But he knew the mission would be easier if Diana were part of it. One smile from her and he forgot to worry about himself. That was real magic.

Just wish she was here now, he thought, then he slipped into the shadows behind the rest of the team. *I hope that wherever she is, she's safe.*

As Sammy moved with the team, he thought of Diana. Steve hadn't offered any explanation for her absence, but somehow Sammy knew that she was all right. Indestructible was more like it. His eyes crinkled and he sent her a silent message: *Wherever you are,* bonne chance, *chérie.*

Good luck.

And then he saw something that suggested their own luck had changed.

This dark world had just become darker. Beneath glowering storm clouds, sharp winds building around her as the first few drops of rain blew sideways, Diana jumped back down to the balcony of the control tower with the Godkiller in hand. Now she could take him on. She regarded Sir Patrick through the glass. There was nothing about him that would have revealed him as Ares except for his own arrogant boasting. *Nothing.*

"I am not your enemy, Diana," he said. His newly strengthened voice carried over the howl of the wind. "I am the only one who truly knows you. And who truly knows them." He paused as if measuring her reaction. "They have always been and always will be weak, cruel, selfish, capable of the greatest horrors."

For the first time, the Godkiller felt heavy in Diana's grip. She took the sword in both hands, squeezing hard. She would face him down. One on one, as she had taken on so many enemies before. Her mission was just, and she held the weapon that could finish him. She must be brave. She must be the warrior Antiope had trained her to be. She must not fail.

But as she entered the room, Sir Patrick vanished into thin air. One moment he was there. The next, he was gone.

Oh high alert, she scanned the space, skin prickling, heart pounding.

"I am Diana of Themyscira, daughter of Hippolyta," she proclaimed, more to remind herself of who she was and why she was there than to honorably identify herself to her adversary.

His disembodied voice bounced around the room. "All I ever wanted was for the Gods to see how evil my father's creation was. And they refused."

"And I am here to complete her mission," she declared, ignoring him.

Then he reappeared, the same older man with the aristocratic English name. She aimed the point of her sword at him. One perfectly timed thrust of the Godkiller and it would be over. She took a quick breath, preparing herself for the attack. She would not leave here until he was dead.

Ares simply held up his hand, and the sword's exquisite blade disintegrated in a puff of dust, right down to the hilt. She stared down at what she held in her hand and staggered back, her eyes full of disbelief. He had just destroyed the only weapon forged to kill him.

"The Godkiller," she gasped.

"'The Godkiller?' Oh, child. *That* is not the Godkiller." He shook his head, seemingly in commiseration, and then with two words delivered an even greater shock. "*You* are."

He stepped past her, out the door onto the balcony, and she backed away, every sense screaming danger, telling her to get out of there.

"Only a *God* can kill another God," he said, as if such a thing was common knowledge.

"I?" She didn't understand what he was saying. *She* wasn't a God…

He raised a brow. "Zeus left the daughter he had with the Queen of the Amazons as a weapon to use against me."

To use…

A weapon to use…

As if she were underwater, she heard her mother's voice: *I made you from clay and begged Zeus…* No, it could not be. She was not the daughter of a God. Not a weapon. Not this *thing's* sister—

"You lie!" she cried, reaching for the lasso on her hip.

19

On the airfield, Sammy, Charlie, and the Chief quickly put on the uniforms and masks of the unconscious soldiers Sammy had spotted. Costumed from head to foot, they would blend in perfectly. No one would realize they were undercover enemy soldiers until it was too late—perhaps, with any luck, not even after the mission was complete. What happened next could not matter. What was important was what was happening *now*.

Able to walk freely, they rapidly progressed around the side of the hangar toward the big black plane. It was massive. No one gave them the slightest notice or challenged their right to approach it.

Steve pointed with two fingers, and Sammy moved quickly to the cargo door and disappeared through it, into the fuselage. Steve rounded the nose of the behemoth, taking in its position relative to the other planes on the field and weighing the odds that it could make a successful emergency takeoff. It was possible, he decided, depending on the weight of the bomb load and the side wind conditions. As he returned to the flank of the plane, he saw the Chief peel off from where he stood with Charlie, darting inside the gaping hangar.

Inside the plane, Sammy moved past the neat rows of tightly packed gas bombs and shifted to a position where he could watch the workers load even more without getting in their way. Did any of these people realize what would happen if this plane went down? Doomsday, pure and simple. It was insanity to move such a huge quantity of gas like this. Had they even considered the danger, or did they care? So many thousands if not hundreds of thousands of German soldiers had already died—fodder for the ambitions of the Kaiser.

Around him, more bombs came aboard. Sammy was grateful for the gas mask, even though it smelled horrible and was baking hot. The mask concealed his revulsion and his nervousness. He had been on many missions with Steve and the team, but his silver tongue was his best weapon. The necessity of silence put him off his game.

He kept watching, studying the plane's innards, drawing a mental diagram he could relay to the others. Wires, levers, room for the whole team aboard—

And then his heart jumped into his throat.

A mechanical timer was wired to one of the clusters of bombs—something they'd need to detonate the explosives if they didn't intend to drop them. If they intended to set the bombs off in mid-air.

Over a target.

A city.

Filled with innocents.

Dear God in heaven.

* * *

In his German uniform, the Chief moved unremarked through the hangar to the map of Europe pinned on the wall. There was a big X marked over London, England.

Their target.

His blood turned to ice. That was where the bomber was going. They were going to drop the bombs on a densely populated island from which there was no escape, not for military personnel or civilians. Infants, mothers, grandfathers. The King of England himself. Where they could kill over seven million people. A massacre. If he and the team didn't stop it, this truly would be the War to End All Wars.

No one must drop those bombs. No one.

The team had a new objective.

And failure was not an option.

Acting as if he knew what he was doing, and that what he was doing was absolutely necessary, Steve climbed up on the lower wing of the bomber and pried open a panel on the exterior of the fuselage. His goal was sabotage, and he was looking for cables he could cut, something that would wreck the flight controls.

The panel opened onto a fairly deep enclosure, but there were no cables inside, no fuel lines either. He had studied the plans of all the known German warcraft, but this gigantic bomber was a big unknown.

A muffled voice from behind him said something in German. He pulled his head out and looked down at a soldier holding a Luger pistol. Steve couldn't hear the words, and before he could respond anyway, the German raised the pistol and took aim at Steve's chest.

Charlie moved in behind the German and brought down the steel-shod butt of his sniper rifle. It made a clank against the back of the man's helmet; the Luger and his head hit the ground at the same instant. Steve nodded his thanks.

Hoisting the body up between them, they began to carry it into the hangar. It looked like two German soldiers helping a third who had passed out or was injured. As they neared the hangar's doorway, a chill, steady wind began to rise. It buffeted the legs of their trousers.

As they stepped under the towering doorway, Steve glanced over the back of the unconscious man and saw Dr. Maru and a squad of soldiers walking purposefully across the airfield toward the bomber. Sammy was still inside! Steve and Charlie hurriedly dumped the soldier out of sight.

Steve exited the hangar, waved an arm over his head to get the Chief's attention, then gave him the hand signal for withdraw and regroup. The Chief complied, then stuck his head into the cargo hold, and in seconds he and Sammy were moving at a brisk pace around the front of the plane. As they walked away from the bomber, Maru and her entourage arrived at the cargo door.

When the team reunited, Steve waved everyone back into the shadows. For the moment, they could only watch and wait.

I? The daughter of Zeus? He must be lying.

Diana swirled the Lasso of Hestia once overhead,

then threw it over Sir Patrick's head. He made no attempt to avoid it, and as the loop dropped around him, it glowed brighter than she had ever seen. It was nearly blinding.

"I compel you to tell me the truth!" she shouted at him, jerking the noose tight around his chest.

The lasso's golden energy coursed back and forth between them as he gazed into her eyes. "I am," he said flatly. "What I'm saying is true. I am not the God of War, Diana. I am the God of Truth. Mankind stole this world from us and ruined it day by day. And I, the only one wise enough to see."

He put his hands on the lasso. Energy shot through it and burst into Diana. His voice filled Diana's ears as the vision faded. "I was too weak to stop them. All these years I have struggled alone, whispering into their ears. Ideas, inspirations for weapon, formulas."

Suddenly Diana saw Dr. Maru in her laboratory, her worktable strewn with balled-up pieces of paper. Then Ares/Sir Patrick glided past her, whispering into her ear. Maru's face lit up and she plucked one of the wads of paper, unfolded it, and smiled. She mouthed the words, "I've got it. I've got it."

Ares spoke again to Diana. "But I don't make them use them. They start these wars on their own. All I do is orchestrate an armistice I know they cannot keep in the hope they will destroy themselves."

The God's goal was to bring about the end of the world, just as Steve had told the Amazons back on Themyscira. When she had left in search of a monster...

...and found her destiny.

The wind whipped around the control tower, gusting

through the open window, making the entire structure sway. Diana stood fast, one end of the Lasso of Hestia in her hand, the other around Ares' chest—crackling and snapping with golden energy. He clutched the lasso; instantly they were transported to No Man's Land and the full horror of the war. Proof of mankind's ability to turn on itself. All around them: apocalypse, madness, all caused by mankind, incapable of stopping themselves from destroying each other—and the beautiful world.

As suddenly as she and Ares had appeared at the Front, she saw Ares, younger, more vital, in the battle armor of the ancients surrounded by lightning and thunderbolts, power such as she had never seen. Locked in combat with the King of the Gods; then Ares falling backwards. Next, Ares as he appeared now—a mortal man who had aged, crouched huddled in a cave, shivering, without clothing, and alone.

"But it has never been enough until you. When you first arrived, I was going to crush you." He let that sink in before he continued. "But then I felt something I haven't felt for thousands of years." He waited another beat. "*Stronger*. And I knew that if you could see what the other Gods could not, then you would join me and with our powers combined, we could finally end all the pain, all the suffering, the destruction they bring."

Instantly they were transported to a beautiful, lush forest unsullied by war, no sign of people anywhere. She smelled the fresh earth and sky, felt the radiant sunlight on her face. It was as perfect as Themyscira. Then he took them to the horror of No Man's Land—gray, stark and devastating.

Then they were back at the airfield. Ares ran his finger along the lasso, toying with it. Golden energy arced into that finger; it flowed up his arm, shoulder, and neck. He was feeding on it. He was glowing, transforming…

"It is because of you," he said with a smile. Golden light shone behind his teeth. "All of these years, I've been struggling to regain my power, to cleanse the Earth of the blight of man—only to realize that the very weapon my father created to *destroy* me… not only could restore me to the God I once was, but was actually the thing I needed most."

Diana's pulse pounded in her temples. She didn't understand, but she desperately needed to. The King of the Gods and her mother… Hippolyta had given birth to her in the ways of mortal women? Could this actually be true? If that was the case, every single Amazon on Themyscira must have known as well. Why had she, Diana, not been told? How could her mother send her to the world of men without telling her?

I am the daughter of a God? She tried to believe it, tried to make the pieces fit. Zeus was Ares' father, too. Was she then this monster's half-sister? *That cannot be. I was born into a community of peace-loving warriors. My essence is not the same as Ares the War Glutton, the Curse of Men.*

Trembling at the thought, she kept a firm hold on the lasso. Then fire erupted from his hands. He turned them back and forth, examining them, and he ran them hand along the magical rope. Energy crackled; the lasso threw cascades of sparks onto the floor. He grinned at her.

He's trying to confuse me. He is the Father of Lies.

"We could return this world to the paradise it was before them," he said. "Forever."

Once again, they stood in the sweet, green forest—devoid of man and all his atrocities. Without men, the entire world would look like this. Without them—

"I could never be a part of that," she told him, her tone defiant.

He sadly shook his head. "My dear *sister*…"

He returned them to the control room. "I don't want to fight you." Then his face hardened. "But if I must…"

He grabbed the lasso with both hands. A tremendous blast of energy erupted from the rope, from within him; it billowed like a fireball, engulfing the control tower. In the next fraction of a second the entire building exploded, sending its zigzag support struts flying. Without the supports, there was nothing to hold the structure's tall legs together, and they buckled and gave way. The ruins of the tower fell to earth in a sickening rush, crashing on the ground and shattering. Diana fell along with the mass of debris, landing in a smoking pile of it; the impact knocked the breath out of her.

The airfield was rocked by a deafening explosion; Steve and the others were thrown to the ground. *They've detonated the poison bombs,* Steve thought. But if that had been the case, he would be dead.

German soldiers scattered in a panic. The compound was under attack, but from whom and where? There had been no sound of an aircraft flying overhead, so it couldn't have been an Allied bomb. There had been no distant boom of a cannon, so it couldn't have been an artillery shell. It was conceivable that the explosion was an accident.

An accident at a site that stockpiled the most deadly weapon ever devised. That was something even more terrifying. The Germans pulled their gas masks tighter on their faces, making sure they had a good seal. But Steve had seen Veld. The destruction had been near-instantaneous.

What if it had been Maru's lab? He pictured poison gas billowing overhead, riding the wind across Belgium. He had no idea if the masks they wore would keep out the gas or they had been designed to protect the rank and file.

When the shaking stopped, he signaled to his team and they raised their eyes to the airfield, the night sky. There was nothing on their side of the airfield. Deeper reconnaissance was in order.

On Steve's command, they rushed into the darkness.

When the shock wave hit, Dr. Maru was caught out in the open beside the new prototype Zeppelin-Staaken long-range bomber. The heavy aircraft's tail lifted in the air and its nose dipped down, but its wheels did not come off the ground. She was thrown head over heels and as she rolled, she grabbed hold of the edge of the lower wing and hung on for dear life until the blast of pressure passed. She stood with shaking knees as the flight crew staggered out of the cockpit in a daze.

Her lab had not exploded, of that she was certain. They were under attack, probably from enemy aircraft flying above the cloud cover and using the thunder to conceal their engine noise.

There would be no scheduled flight check now. She had to get the bomber's precious cargo out of harm's way and in the air without a moment's delay.

She gestured for the crew to go back into the cockpit and shouted a command to take off. "Go!" When they hesitated, she yelled, "Get this plane out of here!"

Dazed, Diana pushed up to a sitting position on the smoldering heap of metal, her cheeks and fingertips tingling from the initial blast of heat. Ordnance, vehicles, and debris littered the airfield from one end to the other.

Ares was nowhere in sight. For a moment she wondered if he'd been vaporized by the blast of energy. Then she looked up. High overhead, the being she once knew as Sir Patrick was slowly floating down to earth.

He has the gift of flight, she thought. *Because he is a God.*

"Oh, my dear," he drawled as she jumped to her feet, cleared the fiery debris pile in a single bound, and charged at him. With the sheer force of will, he lifted the tower wreckage, molded it into a single blazing mass, and threw it into her path. "You still have so much to learn."

Diana dodged the fragments falling all around her and threw her lasso at Ares—but he held up his hands and blasted it back. Whirling it overhead, she lassoed a massive chunk of debris and heaved it at him—but before it could hit him, he rose straight up in the air, out of its path. The chunk of rubble smashed into a fuel tank, and it exploded with a withering blast of heat and flash of orange light.

The battle was on. Adding to the challenge, the storm had peaked. A furious wind whipped over the airfield, buffeting Diana back and forth, making her hair stream behind her like an ebony pennant. In the wild fluctuations of air pressure, the lasso went taut, then loose. She pushed through the gale, advancing toward him as he hovered in mid-air, his hands raised like an orchestra conductor. At his command, enormous chunks of tarmac ripped up from the airfield. They flew at her like missiles. She avoided one huge piece, then smashed through another, sending fragments in all directions. Then a massive slab of earth broke free, and began to rise.

Diana leaped into the air, straining for maximum altitude, and when she reached the apex, she hurtled down, aiming for Ares.

Winding their way through the pandemonium, Steve and his team fought the wind and the explosion's aftershocks that rippled through the ground underfoot. What with the fire, the wind, and the upheaval, it felt like the end of the world, something Steve was familiar with—he had fought at the Battle of Passchendaele, where six hundred and fifty thousand troops had lost their lives.

They hustled behind a hangar, removing their masks. Then they looked up, and Steve's mouth fell open. Above the field, a man was suspended in the air, floating like a balloon as the wind screamed around him. *Who's that?*

Is he suspended on wires? But that's impossible. There's nothing to be suspended from. Above him there was only churning black sky.

However he had accomplished it, the man had broken the bonds of the Earth and Diana was battling him. The airfield was being torn up by invisible forces, great chunks of it simply flying up out of the ground and zooming at Diana. She dodged, them, leaping, crashing her fists into them. She was in tremendous danger, and yet, with her glowing lasso and shield, she was holding her own.

Then a massive section of earth rose into the air. It was enormous, bigger even than a football field. Simply rising, as if by magic.

Diana made for her adversary, but he appeared to unleash some kind of tremendous power from his hands. It blasted her back and positioned her under the hovering plate of earth. He motioned like a magician, sending the enormous object crashing to the ground. In a blur, just before it hit, she zipped out from under it and slammed into Sir Patrick, sending him flying. Steve was dry-mouthed, speechless, scarcely able to believe what he was seeing.

"Oh, my God, what do we do?" Charlie asked.

"There's not much we can do if that's who I think it is," Steve said slowly. He was stunned almost to speechlessness. Was she actually battling Ares, the God of War?

As they gaped at Diana, the truck that towed the enormous black bomber began to strain forward. Steve tore his attention from Diana's battle in the sky and focused on the plane, crammed to the gills with poison gas bombs. Maybe they couldn't stop a God. But they were still in the game, and they had to do whatever it took to make sure the good guys won.

"We can stop that plane," Steve said, and from the expressions on their faces, the others had had the identical thought.

"What if we radio ahead?" Charlie said. His face had turned so red he looked apoplectic. "They could shoot it down."

Steve shook his head. "It crashes, it wipes out everyone around. We have to ground it."

Sammy grimaced. "If we ground it here, same thing. It'll kill everyone for fifty square miles."

He's right, Steve thought dismally. They were at an impasse. *We can't let them fly it over England, and we can't leave it on the ground here either. But we have to do something.*

An idea formed.

"It is flammable, Chief?" Steve asked. Among them, the Chief was the technician. Charlie was the sharpshooter, Sammy was the smooth-talking persuader, and the Chief made explosives—witness the tomahawk special he had used in Veld against the Germans.

"Yeah, she said it's hydrogen," the Chief replied, meaning Diana. "It's flammable."

Steve had part of the answer, then. He was pretty sure his plan would work. And if it worked, then— He felt a fillip of fear, tamped it down.

That's all that matters. That it works.

"I need you guys to clear me a path to that plane."

It took a moment, and then like a fuse igniting three separate targets, they grasped what he was about to do.

"No! Steve!" They protested in a chorus.

But their voices were distant as he put all his focus on the mission. The winds blew as he stared at the plane.

How long can this go on? Diana asked herself.

The Titans and the Olympians had fought without respite for ten years. Time had once had no meaning to the Gods. Thousands of years drifted by as if in a dream. But now her warrior's reflexes were being sorely tested. One instant of poor timing or slow recovery and she could be dead.

She was running out of projectiles to throw at Ares. Darting to the side, she grabbed a massive wooden crate and hurled it at her foe. He raised a hand—and the crate appeared to hit an invisible wall. It burst apart, revealing hundreds of small dark objects inside. She recognized them at once—bombs. So many, too many—she could not let them hurt the mortals on the ground below.

The bombs hovered, jostling each other, for a split second—then Ares sent them down toward Diana. From the litter of ordnance on the ground she picked up a standard-issue bomb and threw it hard. It detonated, exploding all the bombs at once in a deafening thunderclap, sending Ares and her flying backwards towards different ends of the airfield.

Steve saw Diana hit the airfield on her back, then bounce, then roll, bounce, then roll, covering hundreds of feet before sliding to a stop. He left the team and raced to her side. She was lying on her back, dazed, but apparently not seriously harmed.

He closed his eyes and gave heartfelt thanks, to whom or what he was not sure, but it seemed the right thing to do. When he opened his eyes he saw the bomber was still being towed by the truck, slowly dragged in the direction of a clear stretch of runway. German soldiers surrounded it, and Steve's team fought back, outnumbered and outgunned, but his brave men stayed in the game.

Steve helped Diana to her feet.

He's still alive. He's all right.

Steve held Diana, was speaking to her. Her ears were ringing from the force of the explosion. His lips were moving, but she couldn't hear a word he said. But he was here, and he was alive.

"What?" Her voice sounded strange, as if it was a million miles away.

He kept speaking. Very earnestly. He was telling her something important. Perhaps that Ares was dead…

Were those tears in his eyes?

From his vantage point, Charlie yelled at Steve through cupped hands, "Steve! *Now!*"

Gunfire crackled. And powerful engines roared to life.

Steve tore his gaze from Diana and looked at Charlie, who was frantically motioning at the plane—all four of its propellers were madly whirring. While a group of soldiers fired at the team to keep them pinned down, another group had unhooked the shot-to-hell tow truck, and the bomber was rolling forward under its own steam. He had to leave her.

He had to go.

"...Wish we had more time," Steve said to Diana. Her face was a blank. He wanted to tell her a thousand things: to thank her for getting back into the battle; to ask her if it was Ares she was fighting; and he wanted to tell her that he believed in her.

The howling wind, her buffeted eardrums. Diana couldn't hear everything Steve was saying. "...Wish... had... time."

She knew that something was happening. The mission was still in progress. It was important and it was crucial that she hear him and she couldn't.

"No. What are you saying?" she pleaded.

"... it's okay... Save today... You can save the *world*..."

When Steve looked over his shoulder, Diana followed his line of sight. The demonic black plane was turning onto the runway. He took his watch out of his pocket and pressed it into her hand. She glanced down at it; then, he turned and ran towards the slowly moving plane.

Then across the airfield, in the midst of the fiery debris, a shape moved.

Ares.

Debris from the field stuck together and clanked around him as he rose from the flames. He stood clad in full armor—helmet to greaves—and he was stronger, bigger, younger, as she had seen him in the vision of the last battle. Saw her, came for her. She raced to meet him head on.

When she was done here, she and Steve would have all the time in the world.

Her hearing restored, she heard the ticking of his watch.

20

Steve ran up to the team, and the four of them shared a look. They had been through a lot together—missions, brawls, firefights, and dogfights. So much. And now...

Now it was time to do this.

Without another word, they crouched behind boxes and crates to lay down more covering fire as Steve ran toward the plane. Enemy soldiers converged on them, firing as they advanced.

Better at us than at Steve, Charlie thought, as he got off a shot that made its mark. The bullets rained down on the trio. Charlie kept his eyes sharp and his powder dry.

Back in the game, just in the nick.

Steve caught up to the lumbering plane. Prop wash blasting his face, he grabbed one of the bi-wing's guy wires and pulled himself onto the lower wing. He opened the door, to find a German on the other side of it, throwing him an astonished look. Steve grabbed the man by the collar and threw him onto the runway.

* * *

As Diana ran faster and faster, Ares raced toward her. They were two unstoppable forces about to collide. From the fire, Ares manifested two swords and held them in his fists.

The real battle began, a demi-God against a God. They flew at each other over the churning chaos below, through the howling wind.

Something had to break. Someone had to die.

The plane was moving, creeping forward to its takeoff point. The vibration of the engines and the wheels on the tarmac made everything around Steve shake. He moved down the cramped, low-ceilinged central aisle to where the pilot and co-pilot were seated. Spotting him, the co-pilot got up and pulled his gun from his holster, aiming it at him.

The pilot shook his head urgently and pointed at the gas bombs. He said in German, "You hit that we *all* go up."

The crewman nodded and put his gun away. Then he ripped a fire hatchet from its brackets on the wall and charged at Steve swinging it. Unable to use his gun as well, Steve dodged the hatchet, then slammed his fist into the co-pilot's midsection, doubling him over and sending him crashing back against the rows of bombs. Steve followed up, wrestled the hatchet away, and hit him again, and this time the man collapsed on the bomber's deck. The pilot picked up a heavy wrench from the tools strewn about and rushed him. Steve spun away. The pilot tried to backswing into Steve's exposed neck, but he twisted and blocked the blow. The tools clanked together. For a moment they were locked, teeth gritted, muscles straining. Steve could smell liquor on the man's breath. Then the plane hit a pothole on the runway deep enough to rattle the bombs in their racks.

When Steve felt the pilot's balance shift, he waited for the man to overcompensate on the recovery. It was only a fraction of a second, but Steve used it to utmost advantage, pulling instead of pushing, turning aside as he slammed the pilot face-first into the steel deck. The wrench bounced away from the man's hand and he lay still.

Steve tossed away the wrench and rolled all three Germans out of the bomb bay doors. They landed on the tarmac. Then he hurried back to the cockpit. He climbed into the pilot seat, located what he thought had to be the throttle control, and pushed forward on the lever. He wasn't sure what takeoff speed was required, especially with the heavy cargo. He tried to breathe deeply, waiting and waiting, watching as the Belgian landscape blurred and the aircraft shimmied and rattled around him.

When it was do or die, the end of the runway in sight, he pulled back on the yoke, and the black aircraft's wheels slowly lifted off the pavement. Higher and higher the plane climbed, heading straight for the forested hills.

The plane was his.

Realizing that they must abandon the airfield forever, Dr. Maru frantically gathered up her notebooks and papers and fed them to the flames. Ludendorff had gone missing in the hellstorm that had swallowed the compound. She had last seen him on the control tower balcony. If he had been up there when the whole thing blew apart, she had to presume that he was dead. The vials of energizer that she had given him were no defense from that kind of explosion.

The hangar rocked from another blast outside. Boiling flasks and other glassware toppled from shelves and shattered, sending fragments skittering across the concrete floor.

Who is attacking us?

And how?

She still had no answers, but it seemed every inch of the secret base was being destroyed. The flames rose higher as they fed on her records. She reminded herself that the Fatherland had the plane and the bombs. They were what mattered now.

The flames rose ever higher.

While Sammy and Charlie returned fire, the Chief lay down dynamite all over the interior of the hanger. Germany would never build another bomb here. He allowed a brief thought about the Alamo to skirt through his mind, smiled wryly to himself, then continued seeding the structure with more than enough explosives to blow it sky-high. He overturned vats of chemicals for good measure so that they wouldn't blow up from the pressure.

Once done, he set the fuses and ran like hell, dashing to rejoin Sammy and Charlie. The three ducked and covered their ears.

The lab blew apart spectacularly in an enormous ball of fire. The shock wave rolled over them, and then timbers and girders—the heaviest chunks first. They were still falling when bullets began whizzing past their heads. Dozens of German soldiers had surrounded them. Charlie brought his rifle up and fired back. Soldiers toppled. But there were so many of them…

Shooting from the hip, they knew they had to make their shots count, and they did. They were pinned down, and there was no getting away.

21

Gathering speed from the powerful tailwind, Steve pulled back on the yoke, putting the plane into a steep climb. He reached out and tapped the fuel tank gauges with a fingernail. The needles read full. How far from civilization could he get? Could he make it out over the Atlantic? Or would the heavy payload drain the fuel so quickly that he'd crash land on the coast of France? He couldn't come up short, not with so many lives on the line.

The wind ripped at the plane as it continued to climb, buffeting it so violently that the wings flexed and rippled.

An idea popped into his head. If he could climb high enough into the storm, reach the maximum wind stream, if the gas was released then, it would disperse over hundreds, maybe thousands of miles. It would be so diluted that it would be rendered harmless. Pushing the throttles forward to full power, he tried to look out the window but there was no way to see anything. How was Diana doing?

He climbed.

* * *

As the wind tore at Diana, she tore at Ares, landing blow after blow to his head and chest, making him retreat. Behind her, Maru's lab exploded with a rocking boom. Ares fought back and the process reversed—she absorbed the hits while backing up. Then she summoned her strength and countered, sending both of them spinning. He drew back; she deflected an onslaught of debris with her lasso.

Then he was on her, grabbing her by the throat, radiant in his armor, the God of War in his glory, crushing the life out of her and reveling in it as the two flew through the air.

"Is that all you have to offer?" he mocked. Producing a chain, he lashed her wrists, then swung her around, smashing her into a German tank. Ares raised it in his hands like a child's toy, and with a single jerk ripped off one of the treads. When he threw the massive strand of linked steel plates at her, it wrapped around her and slammed her to the ground.

He loomed above her. "It is futile to imagine you can win."

Wrists bound, she struggled beneath the weight, surprised to find that she couldn't move.

Click. The sound of a firing pin hitting an empty chamber. Out of ammo, Charlie leaned his weapon against the crate and pulled out his trench knife. Sammy and the Chief ran out of bullets shortly after.

When their firing stopped and didn't resume, the Germans began to close in.

The team was trapped.

Still struggling beneath the weight of the metal, Diana heard the sound of a plane and looked up into the sky. Dread flooded her veins. Steve had climbed aboard that plane; he had to be the one flying it. The storm was battering it. She knew he had never flown such a craft before. He must be planning to take it somewhere, land it, hand it over to the English…

…*But then why is he climbing so high and so fast?* He was screaming toward the moon like an arrow shot from an Amazon's quiver. *What is he doing?*

And suddenly she knew his plan.

In the cockpit, Steve was focused on the altimeter's needle. It was nearing the mark for 17,000 feet. The engines were starting to misfire badly; the intermittent power loss made the plane shudder and wobble. It felt as if a horse was sitting on his chest; his breathing was hard and fast and he couldn't manage to fill up his lungs. Waves of dizziness swept over him. He smiled. And then he laughed. He felt a little crazy.

I'm running out of air.

It's time then.

With numbed fingers he took his pistol from its holster and pointed it at the bombs. He chuckled to himself. He wasn't afraid. But he was wistful. He wanted to show Diana the beautiful parts of this world. To share it with her. Newspapers and breakfasts. It was not to be.

It was not to be.

Still, he couldn't stop smiling when he thought of her, and of what he was doing, and what this would mean for the world: Peace.

The world was going gray. He was getting loopy. He closed his eyes and pulled the trigger and as he did he said…

High above Diana, miles up into the sky, there was a brilliant flash of light. So bright that it penetrated the storm clouds. Then a roll of thunder louder than anything the storm had produced. The fireball winked out, swallowed by the black sky.

And then there was silence.

She *knew*.

The plane. Steve.

From her lungs came a scream of such grief and rage that the stars in space trembled. The scream was like a living thing, clawing at the sky.

She exploded, a half-God bent on vengeance, and in one savage push, she freed herself from the tire tread wrapped around her. Astonished at her display of power, Ares stumbled back.

Diana lifted her face, tears streaming down her cheeks. Now the storm broke out in full force, raging around her, as if it had been waiting to be unleashed by her wrath; she stood in the center of it. Ares was looking on, smiling in triumph. He crackled with lightning, raising his hands. At his command dozens of lightning strikes hit the airfield. Everything was exploding: buildings, trees, planes.

She whirled around to take it all in. When she

turned back, Ares had disappeared. Ahead of her, she saw German soldiers closing in on her friends—Steve's people—and she transformed into a Fury, an unfeeling machine of death. There was no conscience, no empathy to stay her hand. She moved through the gray uniforms in a dead run, faster than they could follow, faster than they could react. With fists and feet, she broke them. Snapped them like twigs and hurled their bodies into the air. Not just the ones who tried to kill her. The ones who tried to run away. There would be no surrender, no mercy. None would escape. She grabbed the last soldier by the leg and flung him, cartwheeling, into the side of a building. Lungs heaving, she let out a piercing cry of triumph.

Then in a voice that bombarded her from all sides, Ares said, "Look at what you've done."

She turned, searching for him. Then overhead, thunder boomed from the dark swirling clouds. Flames and destruction raged around her as the voice rang out again:

"Look at yourself. You came here, Diana, with such determination and hope…"

Panting like an animal, she tried not to listen. And then she saw him ahead of her, silhouetted by the roiling clouds. She thought of all the horrible things she had seen in Man's World—mud-splattered, hollow-eyed children; mothers reaching out their hands for a crust of bread; stumbling old grandfathers forced to build the bombs that would obliterate their villages. Death and destruction. The antithesis of everything she had known on her island.

"And look at you now. Mankind did this to you. Not

me. Weak, just like your Captain Trevor. Gone and left you nothing, and for what? Pathetic. He deserved to burn."

Bellowing in rage, Diana executed a front flip and tackled him, punching him with her fists. Hard, harder. She lifted a tank over her head. Ares turned toward the runway, toward a military transport truck that was speeding away from the compound. His hand twisted at the wrist and the winds suddenly shifted. He was manipulating them, using them to lift the vehicle to fly off the ground and send it spiraling at Diana. She dodged it. It crashed to the earth, but still kept coming, flipping end over end and breaking apart. Dr. Maru tumbled out of the wreckage, sprawling at Diana's feet beneath the upheld tank.

"Look at her and tell me I'm wrong," Ares taunted her, urged her.

Dr. Maru. Mass murderess. A monster who had laughed as men choked and gasped in her torture chamber. Who had sent bombs to the Veld just to make a point.

Diana stared in abject hatred at the evil woman. She wanted to crush her.

I will kill her. It's the least that I can do for this world.

Dr. Maru put her hands up, cowering, her metal mask flapping off in the wind, leaving her grotesque and pathetic.

"She is the perfect example of these humans," Ares declared. "Evil. Corrupted. Unworthy. End her, Diana," he cooed.

Diana stood surrounded by the carnage she had wrought and the wreckage Ares had created—

destructors, the both of them. War drums thundered in her soul. Steve was dead. And this woman's blood was on his hands.

"*Do it!*" The God of War commanded.

She held the tank overhead, her anger threatening to overtake her. Her hatred.

Then the image of Steve's face filled her mind. Their last moment together, when she had been deafened by the shower of simultaneous grenade explosions, replayed from the beginning. Now she heard him speaking; she heard it all for the first time:

"*I'm sorry I didn't believe. But I'd given up believing in so much.*" His voice caught. "*Until I met you. From the first day I saw you, you were everything I ever wanted to believe in. You can do this, Diana. I know you can.*" He paused, eyes glistening. "*But I have to go.*"

"*What?*" she cried.

"*Now!*" Charlie yelled.

He looked over at the team, then back at her. "*I wish we had more time.*"

"*No,*" she said desperately. "*What are you saying?*"

"*It's okay. This is what I came here to do. I can save today, but you… you can save the world.*"

He pressed his watch into her hand. She looked at it, confused, then looked up to see him running away.

His face reappeared—one last look, lingering, regretful. His heart was breaking. She focused hard, choking back sobs, and heard his voice all around her:

"*I love you.*"

Then she was back in the present, an Amazon again, and not the half-sister of the craven murderer of their father.

I am an emissary of peace. I am not a wanton killer.

She realized then that she was under Ares' spell. She was caught in his thrall. His poison was filling her mind, her heart, and her soul. She was not a creature made for vengeance. She had been created to bring harmony to mankind. To show them love. She looked at Maru, trembling and panting.

Dr. Poison, terrified, and alone.

And in that moment, she grasped what Steve had been trying to tell her: that, yes, mankind possessed the ability to be destructive, and cruel—but there was goodness in them that could be nurtured, and could grow—that no matter their flaws and shortcomings, they had the capacity to act through love—to be selfless, and kind, and heroic.

To be like Steve Trevor.

Was it the foreordinance of the Amazons to punish humanity for its shortcomings?

"No," Diana said quietly to herself.

When she opened her eyes, they gave off a golden glow. She had been transformed; she knew what love was. Power thrummed through her as never before. It was so strong. It was more than hatred. More than compassion. It was a force unto itself, and the strongest weapon that she could wield.

"You're wrong about them," she told Ares. She lowered the tank. Dr. Maru stumbled to her feet and fled.

Thwarted, he exploded into a snarling, vicious rage, filling the sky with ash and storm. He raised his hand and launched a storm of swords at her—hundreds of them—but she deflected them with the blast from her crossed bracelets.

"No!" Ares howled.

"'And they were created in his own image,'" she said, reciting the story her mother had told her so many times. "'They were fair and good, strong and passionate.'"

She walked calmly toward the God, her own power now transforming the storm into harmless gentle rain, as if her very presence was negating his power.

"Lies!" he shouted. Seething with fury, he gathered up the wild storm clouds and within them the fury, power, and majesty of Zeus's own heavens, and hurled them at her. But they dispersed harmlessly against her once more.

She said, "'The Gods made us, the Amazons, to influence men's hearts with love and to restore peace to the world.'"

"Love?" Ares scoffed. "The love my father gave them? The love my father *never* gave *me*!"

His shimmering horned form revealed itself, hovering around him like a ghost. His attempted blow did nothing, and Diana continued walking toward him.

"I saved them once," Ares said. "But they didn't deserve it. They do not deserve your protection."

And the words of Steve Trevor echoed through her voice: "It's not about what they deserve. It's about what you believe."

And I believe in love, thought Diana.

Ares crackled with lightning. The blaze coursed down his arms, coalescing in his hands. Again there was a shimmering of his true form and then it was gone.

"Then I will destroy you!" he shrieked.

Diana leaped into the air as he unleashed a massive lighting blast, not just one strike but hundreds, a barrage like no other. It came at her and came at her and came at her as the bullets and the mortars and the soldiers had come at her; as grief had come at her, and as hatred. Hitting her over and over in retaliation—his vengeance, his grief—a tidal wave of the pent-up fury of a God whose own creator had despised him.

Absorbing the heat and the force, Diana pressed closer, then she swung up her arms and crossed her bracelets in mid-air.

"Goodbye, brother," she said.

Boooooosh! Ares's final barrage of lightning hit them; they glowed blue and she grimaced against the searing pain. She held the pose, held it, and held it until, like the release of a coiled spring, the full force of the energy, more powerful than all the bombs ever made, shot back into Ares. His scream was like that of ten thousand men. Then he burst apart in a blaze of light that shook the world, and cratered the ground below.

The God of War was no more.

Dawn.

The rain washed the blackened smoke from the sky, and rosy colors of sunrise washed the world. Soldiers were rousing as if awakening from a nightmare—the better side of man was returning. They pulled off their gas masks like players in a Greek tragedy. Diana did not see Dr. Maru among them.

Charlie, Sammy, and the Chief stood together, still alive; the Germans were leaving them alone. Then they began shaking hands. Helping one another. Leaving the war behind.

A last flake of ash swirled around the Daughter of Zeus and Hippolyta. She lifted her head to the breaking sun. And in the surround of silence, she heard a greater silence.

Steve's pocket watch had stopped ticking.

EPILOGUE

"Some say an army of horsemen,
some footsoldiers, some of ships,
is the fairest thing on the black earth,
but I say it is what one loves."

—Sappho

Wonder. Such wonder.

All over the world, church bells pealed and huge throngs cheered, and laughed and danced in the streets. The Great War, the War to end all wars, was over. And in Trafalgar Square, London, wonderful chaos overtook humanity like a wild bacchanal. Confetti and streamers seeded the sky with joy. Flags whipped in the breeze. Horns and brass bands cheered soldiers wearing crowns of flowers, grabbing pretty nurses for a kiss. Drums thundered, but they were not war drums. They were the chants, the rhythms of peace.

Diana and Etta Candy walked together toward the packed square. Diana was dressed as Diana Prince, hair up, glasses on. Etta had put on something new and pretty for the occasion, and they took in the joy of the celebration.

Charlie, Sammy, and the Chief joined them. Together they reached the recently erected wall of war memorial photographs, photographs of the fallen warriors who had given their lives in defense of England and her allies. Flowers, ribbons, and notes were attached to the lists.

And there he was. Diana's throat tightened as she spotted Steve's photograph. A slightly younger Steve in a pilot's flight gear standing beside a plane. So dashing and happy, eager for his life to begin. So very much alive.

Tears welled; she smiled through them as she touched the picture. Steve had loved her, and he was gone. But the love that he had kindled inside her had not gone. It had grown, and it encompassed all of humanity. These cheering people, this planet of wonder.

Paris
The Present

Power.
Grace.
Wisdom.
Wonder.

I used to want to save the world, Diana thought.

A hundred years later, she was standing in her office in the Louvre, gazing at the photograph she had originally tried to steal from Lex Luthor. She had discovered that he had already known about her and had been collecting information on her, and had somehow acquired the photo. She wanted the sepia print of Charlie, Sammy, the Chief, Steve, and her, in the little town of Veld, for a far more sentimental reason. It was that attempt to take the photograph from Luthor's headquarters that had tipped off Bruce Wayne—Batman—that she was not of this world. Not precisely, anyway.

To end war and bring peace to mankind.

Her gaze lingered on the image of Steve. The people in the photograph were dead now. They were mortals, subject to the commands of time. If only she and Steve had had more of it.

But now I know… I've touched the darkness that lives in between the light. Seen the worst of this world, and the best. Seen the terrible things men do to each other in the name of hatred… and the lengths they'll go to for love.

Now I know. Only love can save the world.

She took a breath.

She lifted Steve's watch from her pocket, turning it over in her hand, then over again, feeling its smoothness. It had stopped ticking the moment he had died. That moment was frozen now, forever, in time.

She placed the watch beside the photograph, then typed out an e-mail to Bruce Wayne:

Thank you for bringing him back to me.

So I stay. I fight and I give for the world I know can be. This is my mission forever.

Just as she hit send, she heard the wail of sirens. Moments later, dressed in her Amazonian armor, she stood atop a building, scanning the cityscape of Paris. In the distance, flames colored the horizon. A fire. People in danger.

There. Time to go to work.

Wonder Woman leaped off the roof and launched into action.

ABOUT THE AUTHOR

New York Times bestselling author Nancy Holder has written numerous tie-in novels for properties including *Buffy the Vampire Slayer, Angel, Grimm,* and *Beauty & the Beast,* and her film novelizations include *Ghostbusters* and *Crimson Peak.* A four-time winner of the Bram Stoker Award, she is the author of dozens of novels, short stories, and essays on writing and popular culture.

For more fantastic fiction, author events,
competitions, limited editions and more

Visit our website
titanbooks.com

Like us on Facebook
facebook.com/titanbooks

Follow us on Twitter
@TitanBooks

Email us
readerfeedback@titanemail.com